The Asylum

By Zahid Zaman

The Asylum
A novella by Zahid Zaman

© 2016 Zahid Zaman

9780993526565

Published in 2016 by Arkbound Ltd (Publishers)

Sponsored publication.

No part of this publication may be reproduced, stored in a retrieval system, or transmitted, in any form or by any means without the prior permission of the publisher, nor be otherwise circulated in any form of binding or cover other than that in which it is published and without a similar condition being imposed on the subsequent purchaser.

■■■

Arkbound is a social enterprise that aims to promote social inclusion, community development and artistic talent. It sponsors publications by disadvantaged authors and covers issues that engage wider social concerns.

Arkbound fully embraces sustainability and environmental protection. It endeavours to use material that is renewable, recyclable or sourced from sustainable forest.

Arkbound
Backfields House
Upper York Street
Bristol BS2 8QJ
England

www.arkbound.com

Preface

Dare to enter a psychiatric hospital? An environment where you can't be sure who the good guys are and who the bad guys are, where you are never sure what is *really* going on?

Read and be astounded by this incredible story of love, hope, fear and death against the minions of Hell and Lucifer himself. Journey with our hero as he travels into Hell to save his very soul.

St Mark's Psychiatric Hospital is set next to a densely wooded forest, out of sight and earshot of anyone who might happen to be passing by. Patients are bussed in from all over the country.

Why can't their own local hospital take care of these patients? What is it about them that makes them so terrifying?

The Asylum

This is a tale so strange, if someone had told it to me I wouldn't have believed it in a thousand years, but now... Now I know it to be true.

St Mark's Psychiatric Hospital is situated on the outskirts of town, near a densely wooded forest. It is newly built and has clean shiny floors and walls. I remember one of the staff remarking to me once that the place was 'built out of cardboard' and to take a look at it, the walls seemed so flimsy that you might have thought he wasn't mistaken. When you touched the walls, the paint seemed to have an odd-textured feel, like oatmeal, and was thicker than it normally should have been.

There were hundreds of little inconsistencies about the place which should have clued me into the fact that something was not quite right, but at the time I was too enthralled with the whole thing of starting a new job to notice — but I did notice eventually, and I just pray it isn't too late for me to make a difference.

The world is in great danger my friend, a danger so terrifying it chills my blood even now to think of it. I am not being flippant when I say this; I really mean it from the bottom of my heart. But I will get to the danger in good time; first, let me explain the situation and set the background.

My name is Zahid Zaman. I am a 31-year-old psychology graduate from the local university. I acquired a job working at the hospital a few months ago, as a 'health care support worker' or what used to be called a nursing assistant.

Of the seven wards available, I was situated on Ward Four. My ward was designated 'short-term rehab', which meant the patients stay could be anything from a few days to about four years. There were twenty beds, half for male and half for female patients.

Explaining the layout of the ward and the uses to which each room was put is of vital importance to this story. The layout of the ward was in the form of a crucifix, which, oddly, I thought nothing of at the time.

The main corridor was about thirty metres long and two metres wide. The floor was of some sort of shiny laminate material which was an easy-wipe clean surface.

The walls were a clean barren white along which artwork was placed at regular intervals. At the top of the crucifix, just as you entered the magnetically locking double doors, was the office, where the nurses spent most of their time filling in patients' notes and answering phone calls.

Next to the office was the conference room, where we would usually have our afternoon handover, on the opposite side of which was the canteen kitchen, where the patients' meals were prepared.

On the left side of the corridor, next to the kitchen, was the dining room, with a serving hatch. The dining room held six tables with four chairs to each table.

Then, on the opposite side of the dining room, was the 'day room' where most of the patients spent most of their time, next to the conference room. This had about fourteen comfortable chairs, a hi-fi system and a 40-inch plasma screen television. This room led directly onto a large garden and smoking area, which held a small fountain and lots of different kinds of plants and several large ashtrays for the patients to put their cigarette ends in but who, on the whole, tended to just throw them on the floor.

Next to the 'day room' were the male and female toilets, opposite of which was the 'art room', which held a medium-sized six-seater table and a cupboard for art equipment.

Further down, on the right side, was the laundry room where most of the patients did their laundry. Then on the left, further down the corridor and next to the art room, was the clinic where medication would be given out. Next to the clinic on the left were two small doors which opened onto the fire exit.

Just to the right of the fire exit was the nursing bedroom, which had laminate flooring and an en-suite shower and toilet. The patients who were deemed most in need were allocated this bedroom as on the wall was a nurse call button.

Opposite the 'nursing bedroom' was the 'quiet room', a room with two well-stocked bookshelves, three large comfortable chairs and a patients' payphone. Next to the quiet room was the 'robust room' which was just a room completely bare of everything except a large white mattress. This was where we would restrain patients who were getting violent and aggressive.

All the rooms except the kitchens, toilets, art room and clinic had a warm dark brown carpet.

Situated after the quiet room, still on the same corridor, was the crucifix-shaped bedroom layout. Nine male bedrooms on the left, six female bedrooms on the right, and, straight on, four bedrooms which could be either male or female.

My duties initially seemed basic, but that was before I realised exactly what was going on.

I would start a morning shift at 7am, have a five or ten minute 'handover', which basically just consisted of outlining what the patients had been up to and how they had been over the last twenty-four hours. The night shift would then go home and we would start our shift.

Usually there would be four staff per shift, two nurses and two healthcare workers or, as was more often the case, one nurse and three healthcare workers.

The job was fairly simple. Start off by having a cup of tea and general chit-chat about nothing as there would be nothing really much to do until 9am, which was both medication and breakfast time. Sometimes, one of the two elderly patients we had was awake and needed bathing, their minds were so far gone that they were simply incapable of bathing themselves.

Then calling people for their medication at nine o'clock, which usually involved knocking on a patient's door and going into their rooms waking them up, which was called 'running'. The patients on the whole tended to be neutral at best or, more commonly, hostile to this running as they didn't like being woken up at such an early hour.

The ward seemed like its own little world, closed off from the outside world, although most patients were allowed to come and go as they pleased.

As I have already mentioned, there were some strange goings-on which I only became aware of as I worked there over time. For instance, a small bottle of water was kept in the robust room and then there were the staff, the nurses being more mysterious and strange than your normal healthcare workers.

Some of them also seemed stranger than the patients. A lot of them would often chew gum and have a faraway look in their eyes as if they were in another place… Where that place might have been at the time I had no way of knowing.

The paint on the walls had an odd glint to it and was rough to the touch, feeling thicker and heavier than normal paint, but one thing which puzzled me still more was the fact that even the ceilings were painted with the same thick paint.

And then… And then there were the patients, the strangest, oddest assortment of people you could ever hope not to meet, most of which had been brought in, handcuffed, from all over the country. And that was strange, too, their being allocated there from all over the country when their local asylum would have held them probably just as well.

All the staff did shifts, and these were divided into two teams, the 'a' and 'b' teams, the 'a' team would only see the 'b' team at handover for a few minutes, and then not see them again. So you were always working with the same staff, day in day out.

The staff I tended to work with was Leon, a tall broad shouldered staff nurse with an amiable personality and good sense of humour. He had a scar running across his right cheek which he had told me was a birth mark. Leon had gone into mental health nursing straight after leaving college at the age of eighteen and had many funny and interesting stories to tell about the place and the patients.

Then there was Trisha, a large overweight black girl with jagged teeth who seemed to get out of the wrong side of the bed every day of the week. She hardly had a kind word to say about either patients or staff but was someone who knew her job right down to the letter and who you could always rely on in times of need.

Natalie was a mental health nurse, about five feet five with long blond-brown hair, not stunningly attractive but with a heart of gold and a kind, concerned face that just made you want to release all your woes to her.

And then there was me, the fourth and newest member of the team, and a very good additional attachment I might add. However, my employment was in some debate, as can be attested by the amount of time it took for them to inform me whether I had the job or not. I had to wait a full two months before I knew.

My First Day

I arrived early and parked in the car park. It was a cold, foggy and dreary September morning, with the sun yet to peek its head up above the horizon. The **place was as silent as a ghost's tomb.**

I entered the main building, glad to be out of the chilly darkness and into the warm air-conditioned building. The bright lights reflected glaringly off the shiny floors and walls. I descended down a flight of steps and turned right into a corridor which led to the ward and used my swipe pass to let myself in through the double magnetic doors. The lights in the corridor were off and the place reminded me of a graveyard.

The office whose door I now knocked on was small, only about four metres long by three metres wide, and held two desks, two phones, two computers, a large filing cabinet, a smaller filing cabinet, and shelves on the wall stacked with folders, and four comfortable swivel chairs.

The office door opened. I was let in and met by Leon, who seemed to be surprisingly alert and awake for so early in the morning, Trisha, who just sat quietly and looked like she had rushed to get to work and not had time to shower, Natalie, who sat reading a sheet of paper, giving the impression of being the ever-studious nurse, and Daniela, who was about to start handover and had been on the night shift.

I knew that the other healthcare worker who was on with Daniela would be sitting in the dayroom, as there was no need for them to be in handover. Everyone apart from Daniela had a drink of tea nearby or in their hands.

"OK, right, as you're all here," Daniela said in her upper-class accent which I couldn't help but like, "I will start."

She looked at the whiteboard on the wall with all the patients' names and status information on. She whizzed through the twenty patients so fast that I couldn't help but feel that my head was beginning to spin, but everyone else knew the patients well, sat back and took it all in.

"Right, that's handover done," Daniela said, shouting to the other healthcare worker who seemed to appear from nowhere and who I noticed was a short girl with blond hair tied in a ponytail.

"We're off. Come on Rachel," said Daniela after picking up her bag and heading for the door.

And that was that, the night shift were gone, and so went the start of my first day.

The first day passed off uneventfully.

I was slightly disappointed that I wasn't allowed to come out of the office and interact with the patients, as I was made to sit down and read all the policies. File after file of policies, it began to wear my brain down.

At 3pm I finished my shift and, slightly dazed and very confused, found my way to the car park and went home to my one-bedroom flat, where I made **myself something to eat. I tried to relax, which wasn't** easy as the happenings of the day had really gotten deep within my core.

But there was one thing I was sure of and that was I really liked my job, I mean I really really liked my **job and couldn't wait to actually get onto the floor** and meet the patients, and I got my chance the next day.

Handover had finished about half an hour ago and I was sipping my tea and just chatting in the office when I heard a coughing sound coming down the corridor.

Trisha opened the office door and there against the dim light stood a sight I will never forget — an elderly gentleman about sixty to seventy years old, about five foot four with thick scraggily grey hair and a wrinkled face, dressed in green hospital pyjamas which were drenched in urine. The stink brought a pained expression to my face but the others seemed unconcerned.

"Come on Zahid, this is Patrick," Trisha said, showing jagged teeth and her voice scratching and traumatizing my inner ear. She stepped out of the office, putting an arm around Patrick, the patient.

"I will show you how to bath someone."

And so it was that I learnt how to bath patients. It was a simple procedure: ask the patient to get undressed, run the bath, wash their hair with shampoo and dry their bodies with a paper towel, ask them to do their private area, and that was it. In the words of **one of Leon's favourite phrases, 'Bob's your uncle'.**

My second day was much better than my first, although I thought initially that bathing someone was beneath me as I had a degree in psychology.

I did it for the money and the chance to learn new skills and be around people I cared about, especially having spent a short stint as a patient in a similar setting myself.

The other thing I found extremely challenging was at around twelve-thirty — dinner time — all the patients would line up in a queue and wait for their dinner in line but this was usually accompanied by a lot of pushing and shoving and shouting during which time it was my job to keep order. This was no easy task, as at the same time I had to read the menus for the dinner lady so she could put their meals out.

At 9am, 1pm, 3pm and 9pm we had to do what was called a **'fire check' which was basically 'ticking' all the patients in on a chart and knowing in** general where they were in the case of there being a fire.

So that was my job for the first few days. It all passed off uneventfully, but I was enthralled and enchant**ed by it as learning all the patients' names and** reading through their notes to find out their diagnoses was fun and enlightening.

I had seen patients like these before with similar diagnoses but only from a fellow patient's point of view from when I had agreed to treatment voluntarily and spent four months as an 'inpatient', but now I was on the other side of the looking glass, as I imagined one of my favourite childhood authors would have said.

And being on the other side made a world of difference. I had to speak to the patients respectfully and pay attention to what they were saying as not doing so could easily lead to them losing their tempers and taking it out on me or another staff member. With only four staff on and twenty patients we couldn't afford to be casual in our encounters with the patients.

And then one day it happened just as I was beginning to settle on the ward.

I was standing in the corridor listening empathetically to a patient when I heard an ear-piercing whining sound, which I realised was the alarm. I looked to the bottom of the corridor and saw there was a scuffle going on; staff members suddenly rushed past me towards the incident. I saw the patient suddenly disappear in a throng of three other bodies, being shoved and pushed into the robust room.

"Turn it off!" was suddenly shouted up the corridor, and I realised what I was being asked to do. I ran up the corridor with the alarm ringing in my ears, entered the office and turned the reset key in the lock. The alarm suddenly shut off and the ear-piercing siren was replaced by a motionless silence. I stood there for a few seconds trying to catch my breath, and felt my racing pulse and my heart beat in my ears.

After a few seconds I left the office and went to see what had happened. When I got to the robust room, all three staff were standing outside.

"We're OK. Go and keep the other patients away from the robust room and make sure the other patients are okay and don't need anything," said Leon with one arm placed on the door, chewing a piece of gum, the red jagged scar stretching across his cheek. *There's no way I'm going to argue with him*, I thought.

As I turned to go I heard a breathy scratchy voice whisper:

"Was that him?"

"No..."

I turned around but they were silent, just staring at the door with grim contemplative expressions on their faces. I should have realised something was up then but at the time thought nothing more of it and put it out of my mind. Suddenly I heard a loud banging noise and someone shout.

"Bastards!"

The patient was banging on the door.

"Go on. Go take care of the other patients," Trisha said, as Leon opened the door and the three of them entered the robust room.

The Interview

How I got a job in such a strange place is an interesting tale in itself.

The local town held its annual Mental Health Day, during which there were stalls set up advertising the positive aspects of mental health awareness. They also hired some bands to play music.

It was a serene summer's afternoon with hardly a cloud in the blue sky, a gentle breeze blew softly and I was in the company of two beautiful women.

We were all patients at the Jefferson Mental Health Resource Centre and had decided to make it a day out. Jenni was a leggy beautiful brunette who dressed trendily but cheaply as the student she had been until coming down with an almighty bout of depression. She was also a voracious reader and would read late into the night. Me and Jenni really hit it off and became best of friends in a very short space of time.

Dawn was another kettle of fish, she was disturbed in a violent way and had the tendency to let her **emotions take control and lash out at people. I didn't** know what had gone on in her past but I got the **impression it wasn't pleasant.**

"Jenni, I love girls with black hair," I said as we walked up the embankment towards the carnival-like set-up in the centre of town, "what colour's your hair?" I asked, looking at the rich glossy black texture of her hair.

"Mine's very dark brown," she said, looking at Dawn and then they both burst out laughing.

My elation at walking with two beautiful women suddenly dissolved like a soapy bubble in the bath. Seeing my unhappiness, Jenni continued.

"I'm glad I met you Zahid."

"Oh, why's that?"

"Now I can put a name under Z in my diary," and we burst out laughing.

We found all the stalls and heard the music pumping out from the bands and noticed the family-friendly environment with adults and young children walking alongside and looking at some of the circus performers who were also there to raise money for mental health charities.

We found a burger stall and all bought burgers; the taste of fried onions and cooked meat was delicious as we sat down on a bench to eat.

After that I thought it was time to get down to business and went from stall to stall asking if they had any jobs in mental health and eventually one stall gave me a number to ring which I did the following day. I gave my details to the secretary and a few days later received an application form in the post. It was at this time that I was relocating from being an inpatient at the Jefferson Centre to my newly refurbished flat.

As I lay in my flat dreaming of Jenni and wondering whether I would be called for an interview, there was a knock at my door.

I opened it and was happy to see it was my community psychiatric nurse, or CPN as they tended to be called. Raymond came in and sat down and started to ask how I was. I told him I had been 'OK' and was just bored and lonely with my parents having moved out of town to be with my two sisters a few months ago.

"I've got some charts I want you to fill in on a daily basis to plot your progress," he said. I looked them over briefly as he handed them to me.

"Ok, no probs, hopefully this will let me know more about my own illness."

Raymond left and once again I was left with just my own thoughts. I would have liked to ring Jenni but she had moved out of town to restart her degree course and Dawn was someone that I really wanted to avoid if I could.

I thought about my time at the Jefferson Centre and how the staff had been so concerned for me, as at the time I had been diagnosed as suffering from schizophrenia. I thought that demons from the principalities of Hell were vying for control of my soul and thought there was no way out, and that I would have to make a choice between one or the other.

"Jenni, I don't know who to go with," I said as just the two of us sat in the quiet dining room of the

Jefferson Centre. The other eight residents had either retired to the shelter of their bedrooms or were spending the night on leave or in the day room watching the television.

"What do you mean?"

"I think the principalities of Hell are vying for control of my soul and I don't know who to go with," I said, my voice sounding foreign to my own ears. "It's either Beelzebub or Leviathan."

"Well why do you need to go with any of them?" she said, her soft voice caressing the harshness of a tortured mind.

I just swallowed, thinking what a relief it would be to be free from all these crazy thoughts.

"I will pray for you."

We sat in silence for a short time in the dim light of the single ceiling spotlight which we had switched on, our soft breath the only sound.

Jenni and I had made a connection, we had bonded as two lonely souls in need of human warmth and compassion and for that she will always have a place in my heart. Dreaming of Jenni I drifted off into a sound sleep on the sofa of the living room.

I was awoken by the post falling through the mailbox. I went to get it and quickly ripped open the letters; one had the stamp of St Mark's Psychiatric Hospital. I read it eagerly, my eyes scanning the paper and my fingers trembling with excitement and then I saw it: "You have been asked to attend on the 14th of July for an interview for the above post."

"Yes!" I screamed with joy, I had an interview and this could be the beginning of turning my life around.

On the day of the interview I woke up early, about 7am, showered, shaved and dressed smartly.

It was the second time that I had actually got to wear my suit which I had bought a year before for another interview.

I set off at about 9am knowing I had to be there for 9:30. When I got there I parked in the busy car park and found my way to the interview room. We were given a quick simple test to do and then had to wait to be called for an interview.

Eventually after about thirty minutes wait I left the other twelve participants and was called for interview. I entered a small office, the light was shining brightly through the open window and the cool gentle breeze eased my nervousness somewhat.

There were two women, one about fifty-five and one about forty. They sat and started by asking me some simple questions.

"What is your experience with mental health?" asked the older lady with a smile.

"I suffered myself with schizophrenia," I said, "and when I was younger my mother was ill for many years with it too."

They seemed satisfied with that answer and proceeded to ask me several more questions to which I gave the best answers I could. I felt the race of my heartbeat in my ears and clasped my sweaty palms together in an effort to reduce the tension but it was no use.

It was then that I got a strange painful feeling in my leg and felt sick to my stomach.

"I don't feel too good," I said.

"Why what's wrong?" asked the younger woman.

Before I could reply a loud alarm started to ring throughout the building. They looked at each other with concerned expressions and nodded, the meaning of which I didn't fully understand until later... Maybe a little too late. Eventually the interview was over and I breathed a sigh of relief.

I had to wait another agonizing two months before the letter would come through confirming my successful application for the post, during which time I daydreamed about Jenni and fantasised about all the things I would have liked to have said to her if she was near... But she wasn't and my life was empty as a result.

Wednesday

We all sat in handover waiting to start the late shift.

I quickly looked around; there was very little conversation going on beyond the few odd pleasantries which were absolutely essential.

One by one each person made themselves a cup of tea and sat back, waiting for whoever was going to be doing handover from the early shift.

I looked across at Natalie; she seemed to be holding herself tightly together like she was struggling with something or hiding something that she didn't want others to know. I saw Trisha looking out of the corner of her eye suspiciously and, every now and again, quickly looking at Leon and looking away again.

Leon seemed to be in a bad mood, not saying a word to anyone and looking thoroughly grumpy and even angry, like he'd rather be anywhere else but work.

"I've got to go on a special driving course," said Trisha to Leon. Natalie looked up quickly, her blue eyes not revealing anything about what she was thinking except looking worn out and frightened.

"Do yer?" said Leon, not really interested, "what do you need to go on that for?"

"I knocked over an off-duty policeman on his motorbike," she said laughing in her exaggerated manner and showing her jagged teeth.

Natalie quickly looked up. Was that anger I suddenly saw flash across her face or had I just imagined it? It appeared and went again so fast.

"Serves you right then," said Leon, wiping his hand across his face like he was trying to wipe a memory away. "Teach you not to go round knocking over motorbikes."

I just remained silent and looking down. I noticed Natalie looking down also, her face a whiter shade of pale than it had been a few moments ago. She suddenly smiled at me and asked, "Zahid, did you do much yesterday?"

Trying to change the conversation I thought, but not knowing why.

"I just stayed in, didn't do anything at all."

"My insurance is going to be sky-high now I've had this crash, unless I pass this course," said Trisha to Leon, who seemed like he had lost interest in the conversation a long time ago.

"You do anything?" I asked back.

"No, I just went to see a few friends," she said quickly, like a little mouse, I thought, all shy and frightened.

Just then Mat from the early shift came in and sat down, made himself a cup of tea and then proceeded to start handover. Nothing much had happened with the patients, they were all the same today as they had been yesterday and the day before.

Nobody seemed too interested in what Mat was saying and even he didn't seem to be too bothered about it either. He whizzed through the patients and then handover was completed and we exited the conference room and got to work on the ward.

My first task was to sort out **the patients' menus,** my next task was to go and get cigarettes for Patrick, who was running low. The rest of the staff were busy in doing the jobs they needed to do, like ordering medication from the pharmacy for the patients, taking **patients' blood, answe**ring the phone and making appointments with other outside agencies for the patients.

So I was left alone again to simply get on with my job, all the tasks were done without any kind of enthusiasm or semblance interest, we were all there just doing our jobs for our pay cheque at the end of the month.

It wasn't later until medication time at 5pm that I

got a chance to talk to Natalie again.

Trisha was in the day room watching TV, Leon was in the kitchen cooking his tea, and Natalie and I were doing the medication. My job was to call people for their medication after Natalie had their medicine ready and told me who she wanted. Natalie walked to and fro from the drugs cupboard which was on the wall as she doled out the meds.

Some of the patients were reluctant to take their meds as usual but a bit of coaxing by me and Natalie was usually enough to persuade them. In some cases however, as with Patrick, we had to hold him in the chair whilst he took his medication — which was a

Nebuliser inhaler and an anti-psychotic tablet along with something for the side effects of the anti-psychotics — because he would just keep getting up and trying to get away without taking his tablets.

Then after meds it was my job to organise tea-time for the patients, which consisted of standing by the hatch, reading out the menus to the serving dinner lady and calling the patients up for their meals one at a time. But what tended to happen was that more than one patient used to come up at a time and I had to persuade them to go and sit back down, whilst they tried to push and shove each other. It was, I thought, as *if they think someone else is going to steal their food.*

Natalie sat by my side observing the patients and I was glad of her company. I could feel the heat of her nice warm body next to me and it felt very pleasurable.

Then, once the hassle of tea-time was over, Natalie and I started our breaks.

Natalie was rather subdued saying very little and I **didn't know what to say to bring conversation out of** her; she seemed lost in her own thoughts.

I felt happy just to be sitting next to her in the conference room, and noticed how the curves of her hips, waist and chest stood out against her uniform. She caught me looking at her but ignored it and then I **felt like a perv. I hadn't meant to stare at Natalie's** figure but her body being in such close proximity to mine had my mind racing.

We didn't talk much, although I wanted to, I just didn't know enough about Natalie yet to engage her in any conversation.

It seemed that, just like the rest of the staff, she had a lot on her mind. What that could have been at the time I had no way of knowing.

My Work Colleagues

Natalie

Natalie was a hard worker, she had been all her life, and look where it had gotten her — in a job with a high stress level.

And now she was battling depression and post-traumatic stress disorder, the latter only having been **diagnosed a few weeks ago. She hadn't told anyone at** work about her depression or her PTSD but she thought they suspected about her depression.

She knew both problems went back to her teenage years. At seventeen she had been in love with her boyfriend Dave, and then her life had descended into an unbearable hell. Dave was a show-off and his dad was rich.

As soon as Dave passed his driving test on his nineteenth birthday his father had bought him a new car, a Golf GTI, and Dave had taken her for a spin. A spin from which he had never recovered.

He had seen the truck too late and was unable to brake in time. The car ploughed into it, spun, smashed to bits and went up the pavement and then wrapped itself around a lamp post.

The depression was still really bad; even six years later she was still grieving for him. Though counselling had helped, on certain dates or anniversaries her memories and thoughts would come crashing down on her.

At night she used to have flashbacks. Dave was laughing and joking and she was laughing too, the music blaring out of the car radio. The ground whizzing past them at great speed. Then suddenly the **truck came into view; Dave hadn't** seen it.

Natalie had been frozen in shock, wanting to warn Dave but too stricken with fear to say anything other than look in horror and then Dave had seen it but too late. The car had been coming off the slip road and smashed into the truck.

The nightmar**es were still fresh. Therapy hadn't helped much, she hadn't moved on, Dave still** dominated her mind and thoughts.

She had met other men and even lost her virginity to one when she was nineteen but, on the whole it **wasn't that she couldn't feel anything for** them it was just that Dave kept rearing his head from her past and making her feel guilty.

Every time she met a new guy she would at first be excited and then she would remember Dave and guilt and sadness would set in, but it was something she was determined to overcome.

She would continue to have therapy and she would beat her problem. No one knew she was in therapy, not even her mum and dad who she lived with, and no one was going to know. She felt they would see her as weak and, to be honest, she did feel ashamed that she still dwelled on these thoughts so long after the event.

Her two brothers and two sisters had been a great source of support when she was younger but now **they had all left home and she didn't see them as** often as she would have liked.

Leon

Leon awoke, cold and frustrated, in the small dark spare room of their four-bedroom house.

He had been sleeping in the spare room for the past two months, ever since his wife had found out about his infidelity. Now she was filing for a divorce and it was breaking his heart. From the Luminas digital clock on top of his wardrobe next to his bed the time was 4:35am.

His two daughters, who were asleep in the other room and whom he really loved, had sided with their mother in hating him, and it was a pain which he was finding very difficult to bear.

Cold tears dried on his eyes trickling over the scar on his face which now felt cold and icy. He found he **couldn't cry in front of people but now, on his own,** in the dark and cold, he found tears came unbidden and freely.

He had been with his wife for the past 22 years and now that she wanted him out of her life, and that of their children, it was hellish for him. All for one infidelity.

She had been a student nurse, her name was Laura, five feet six, blond hair, fine delicate features, slimly built with a very curvaceous figure and large breasts which had most men staring if not leering at her. She kept herself fit and trim by exercising regularly at the gym and swimming.

Leon had been her assessor, and they had got on well from the start. He had taken her to one side and taught her as much as he possibly could about the mental health system.

To him it was a joke, he had worked in other psychiatric hospitals before coming to this one and realised that most of the time the system was just looking after 'inadequates'. Mummy's boys and people with weak infantile personalities who would rather sit and complain, scream and cry than get up and do something to help themselves.

After twenty years Leon had become disillusioned with the whole system. He was paid to look after and be friends with patients who, in the normal course of life, he wouldn't give two seconds to.

And then he had got his job at St Mark's Psychiatric Hospital and realised how much more challenging and exciting it was. He had loved it from the start, as soon as he had been let into the hospital network he had risen to the challenge, doing risk assessments of the patients and reading into the small hours about Lucifer, good and evil and man's part in the scheme of God's great plan.

Laura... What have you done to me? She had rung his mobile when he had been in the shower and his wife had answered it, asked who it was. Laura had **made some excuse but his wife hadn't bought it; she** had then gone into their bedroom and searched his pockets, finding receipts for restaurant meals.

Laura had soon deserted him after her placement was over. She had, he now knew, only been after a good time and nothing more serious. She had stopped returning his calls when he told her his wife wanted a divorce.

"Not my problem," she had said in that lilting high-pitched feminine voice which he had found so alluring. And that was that, she had ruined his marriage and then left him and his family to pick up the pieces.

The worst of it was that his wife had told their two teenage daughters and the shame of that was something that still burned him.

He had tried to explain how he had been with his wife for the last twenty years and how, over that time, their love life had become stale and dull, with his wife preferring to read a romance novel than to copulate in the shower or get down and dirty in bed, **but they hadn't understood. They hated him and it** hurt.

Laura... if only I hadn't met you.

He looked at the clock, the time was now 5:40; he had been lying in bed for the last hours thinking about his life and what was going to happen to him and his family. It was like this every morning. He would wake up early and spend about three to four hours just thinking about his situation and how miserable he felt.

His wife kept digging the knife in and twisting it, she kept telling him she wanted him out the house as soon as she could and he had agreed that he would go. But now that the time was approaching nearer and **nearer, he realised he didn't want to** leave. He had worked hard for this house and he and his wife had brought up their two daughters here and it held a multitude of memories.

Fresh tears sprang up on his face. He didn't wipe them, he had long given that up, knowing that when he did new ones would only spring up to replace them.

Laura… if only you hadn't been so beautiful.

Trisha

Trisha was angry. Her mother, whom she lived with, often remarked that she was the angriest person she knew. Trisha had been angry from a young age, since her father had left her mother and sister when she was five.

Her anger dominated her whole persona. Her fiancé, who had jilted her and left a few days before **their wedding, had said that he just couldn't put up** with her anger anymore and his leaving had increased her anger tenfold.

She was angry. So bloody angry with men, but her love of her mother and her deep Christian faith, which Trisha had inherited from her, kept Trisha sane and able to deal with day to day life.

And what she thought about the patients she **couldn't tell anyone, for fear of being reprimanded by** her superiors. *Fools, total and utter fools* to have dabbled in the occult and opened themselves up to dark forces. And now, the mental health system and the Catholic Church, they were the ones who would have to pick up the pieces.

They had risked the most precious things they had — their very souls and eternal punishment for a bit of power over their fellow humans.

She knew how it started usually — someone wanting to speak to a recently dead relative or loved **one whose loss they couldn't bear, and then Satan** would entice them in with little snippets of magic and power, a few words spoken by some spirit who would pretend to be the deceased speaking through someone else. Or sometimes it was a love spell, or even a money or power spell.

Greedy people fall into Satan's trap, thought Trisha.

She was 42 now and quickly approaching the menopause, her biological clock ticking away like a time bomb and it seemed, being so overweight, that nobody was likely to appear on the horizon any time soon and she would have to idle away her life as a spinster.

Her anger and hate were colossal, and she knew deep down that she needed therapy but the prospect of it seemed so frightening, like jumping off the tallest mountain into the unknown. She would never **admit it to anyone but she couldn't face it, it was just** too daunting for her. But without therapy it seemed **her anger wasn't going to go away any time soon.**

She had worked at the hospital for six years and did just the bare minimum that her job allowed her to get away with. She had no sympathy for the *fools*, they were there because they had messed up big time **and it was the hospital's job to make sure they didn't** do it again.

Secretly she had always fancied Leon but he had made it clear on several occasions that nothing would be happening between the two of them. This had struck Trisha like a cold knife deep in the heart and sometimes when they would talk, she would think about all the things that she wanted to do with him, and then the knife would twist deeper, though she knew it was lust not love.

Sex... she wanted it so badly but the closest she got was masturbating in the toilet with her hairbrush, something that no one knew, not even her mother who was so close to her.

So that was her life. No wonder she was always in such a bad mood, but one day she thought she would have therapy, and then the weight would fall off her as she'd diet, and then she would meet the man of her dreams. It was a distant hope but it didn't seem to be getting any nearer day by day, and Trisha also knew in her heart that on that day pigs would fly.

A Few Weeks Into The Job

I was on the late shift which was from 3pm to 9:30pm.

Natalie walked up to me slightly hesitantly, it was 6:40pm and we had just finished our evening breaks some ten minutes ago.

"The phone just rang, that was the nursing office upstairs," she said, creasing her forehead in a worried frown. "We got a patient coming in from down south in handcuffs with the police about two hours from now."

"OK," I said, trying not to appear afraid or nervous, although I was.

"He's got a history of violence, so I want you to keep all the patients in the day room and away from him when the police leave him, and until we have him properly assessed by the psychiatrist."

"Sure, I can do that," I said with all the confidence I could muster.

"His notes are in the examination room. His name's Christopher Haunton. If you want you can have a quick read before he gets here so you know what you're dealing with."

"Thanks, I will," I said. Natalie smiled which made me feel surer of myself and then she turned and walked away.

I unlocked the examination room, switched on the light and did the blinds as the darkness scarily stared in at me through the double glazing.

I found the notes, sat at the desk and started to read. Christopher Haunton was well known to psychiatric services, having been admitted to St Mark's asylum on three previous occasions.

First admission at the age of eighteen when he had been found naked in a cemetery with a pentagram etched into his chest and mumbling something unintelligible about demons and Lucifer.

He had been put on a Section 3, and spent six months on the ward during which time he had started several scuffles and fights with staff.

He was 'treatment resistant', which meant he disliked taking his tablets and would often keep them in his mouth and then spit them out when no one was looking.

He also had a propensity to 'avoid bright sunlight' and 'eat raw red meat'. After reading for a while I realised we were dealing with a very strange character indeed.

His mother had died in strange circumstances in what was thought to be a suicide when Christopher was seventeen.

However, Christopher had shown no sadness at the loss of his mother. It was as if he had locked her out of his life and mind and that she, or his memories of her, no longer existed in his world.

There was one odd thing.

Most of the fights, looking at the notes, had occurred around about six o'clock or fairly close to that time.

My mind suddenly started to tick; there was something here which wasn't quite right but before I could dwell on it any further, Natalie poked her blond head and deeply tanned face round the door: "He will be here in ten minutes so if you can get everybody out of the way in the day room, we'd appreciate it," she said with a worried smile, and was gone.

I got up…

Fifteen minutes later I heard the magnetic double doors unlock and two police officers escort a tall well-built scruffy-looking man in his late twenties wearing sunglasses, down the corridor and into the examination room. The police handed over two bags of belongings including clothes and left.

Leon sat in with the psychiatrist as Christopher Haunton was assessed.

Trisha hung around outside the door, listening in case she was needed, and I let the patients go about their normal everyday activities.

After a few minutes I decided to approach Trisha.

"What's wrong with him?" I asked.

Trisha fixed me with a steely glare.

"Stay away from him." Her voice scratched my inner ear.

"What?"

"You will stay away from him, if you know what's good for you," she said as I surreptitiously looked in through the glass panel.

He seemed a little morose and down but not violent or aggressive. On his left finger I noticed several rings and he was still wearing his sunglasses.

Interesting and more interesting, I thought.

The last thing I was going to do was 'stay away from him'. As soon as I got a chance I was going to be in there assessing Christopher and asking questions, when the opportunity presented itself.

Whilst Christopher was in with the psychiatrist, Trisha asked me to take his belongings to his bedroom and write his name and room number down on the fire check-in list.

I wasn't able to garner any more information about my new topic of interest that night as by the time the assessment had finished it was nearly time to go home and Christopher went straight to his bedroom.

Over the next few days it was difficult to engage Christopher in any conversation, as he tended to stay in his room and only come out at meal times and avoid any direct conversation.

I did however notice that Christopher tended to get more agitated at around six o'clock and would start mumbling something incomprehensible under his breath, about demons and Lucifer.

One day as I walked down the corridor I saw him standing in the centre of the corridor and staring at one of the art works on the wall, which I thought was a very dreamy picture of two semi-naked individuals from the top of the chest up with medium to longish hair. It was a very calming piece of work which I thought symbolized first love.

As I walked past he suddenly turned to me with his dark sunglasses and pasty grey skin, and spat through his yellow-stained teeth.

"Do you believe in the Devil?" he asked in a deep intelligent voice which seemed odd to be coming from someone so scruffy and dishevelled.

"What?"

"Do you believe in the Devil?" he repeated more fervently.

I realised the situation could get very ugly quite quickly so with all the sincerity and in the most calming voice I could muster I said:

"I believe other people believe he is real and he has a real effect on people's lives."

That seemed to calm him somewhat, but those sightless glasses with their penetrating starkness continued to stare. Before he could say anything else, I took the initiative and said:

"Hot drinks are out, just go into the dining room and help yourself to a coffee. I'm going to put sandwiches out in a little while."

He continued to stare. I smiled my most disarming smile.

"Go on, you look like you could do with a nice warm drink."

He quickly looked up and down the corridor and then abruptly turned away and shuffled down the corridor to the dining room, all the time mumbling something about Lucifer and demons.

That's one very strange individual; he's definitely in the right place.

On another occasion, during the second week of his arrival, it was about 8:30pm and I saw him sitting in the quiet room alone, going through some books.

Only one light was on and the dimness gave it a cosy comfortable feel.

"Hi, Christopher," I said, noticing the inky black night which threatened to invade the weak light from the ceiling.

He didn't say anything, just continued to stare at a page in a large book he had picked up.

"Is it okay for me to sit in here a while or do you want to be alone?"

No reply. I waited a second and then turned to go.

"You can stay if you like," he said non-committedly.

I smiled inwardly. Slowly, bit by bit, I was breaking down his defences. One way or another I would tear from him the information he didn't want to give me, like the death of his mother and what he was doing in the cemetery naked with a pentagram inscribed on his chest.

I sat down on a comfortable chair opposite him and noticed the book in his hand was the Holy Bible.

I tried to picture his eyes through those dark sunglasses — what colour were they? Were they rheumy like an old man's or were they bright and wide with intelligence?

"It says here that the Great Dragon was cast down from Heaven".

"I've only read bits of the Bible," I replied.

"Don't you think it's a sin to be cast out of your home, never to see it again?"

"Hmm…"

"God started the war but he won't win," his voice rang out angrily. "My lord and master will see to that," he said, suddenly slamming the Bible shut and instantly I felt fear, and a dull throbbing pain in my leg as he now focused on me.

I heard a thump on the window and looked but it was empty, but I felt something there, outside the window trying to get in, something malevolent looking in on me. I felt great danger.

Getting up quickly I said, "I need to go to the toilet," and exited the room as fast as I could.

For a second there I had felt fear, genuine fear, even though I had my alarm strapped to my belt and knew all I had to do was pull it and the staff would come running. I had felt like I didn't want to be in the room a moment longer.

As I exited the room I still felt the dull throbbing pain in my leg and suddenly heard a loud whining sound which rang up and down the corridor.

The staff came running but when they saw nothing was wrong relaxed again.

"You okay?" asked Leon looking down at me, with his scar gleaming in the corridor light.

"Yeah," I responded. "I was just in there with Christopher when I heard something bang on the window."

"The LED on the wall says it's outside the quiet room, it's Zahid's alarm that has gone off," said Trisha, eyeing me with a particularly nasty gaze, her voice sounding like sandpaper across my frightened mind.

"It's okay," shouted Leon up the corridor, "Natalie, turn it off!"

The two of them, Leon and Trisha, started to walk away, and I heard Leon whisper, "My hand hurts."

"My head hurts," replied Trisha. "I think that was him…"

But whatever else was said was just out of earshot.

With the dull throb still in my leg I started my way up the corridor and towards the dining room.

I looked at my watch and with it being 8:30pm I would now have to clear away the supper dishes, empty the tea and coffee flasks, get a tray ready for the night staff which was just a jug of milk, two containers, one for coffee and one for tea, and two cups. After completing these tasks, I would have to do the 9pm fire check-in.

I rubbed my neck with my hand trying to wipe off the unpleasant feeling but it was **no use; it wouldn't** go away.

I spent the rest of my shift staring into the shadows and wondering what was out there, and trying to stay as far away as possible from Christopher.

Maybe Trisha was right, maybe I should stay away from Christopher if I know what's good for me.

As I returned the fire-check to the office a few minutes after 9pm, Leon called me over to him and in **a low serious tone said, "Don't isolate yourself with Christopher Haunton, he's very dangerous."**

I stood looking down at him as he sat on his chair and I saw the scar gleaming across his face.

"OK."

"I'm serious, you could get seriously injured by him before any of us might be able to get there to help you."

I just nodded. "OK," I said again.

Then out of the blue he asked me a question which took me completely by surprise.

"Do you go to the church or the mosque?"

"What? Uh... No, I'm not very religious to be honest with you. Do you?"

Leon didn't say anything, just continued to stare like he was in deep thought.

God, why do you have to be so secretive?

Just then Trisha came walking down the corridor and into the office, and I decided to leave it at that. As

I left I heard Trisha whisper, "I heard what he said. How did he get a job here?"

I looked back and saw the two of them looking at each other with sombre contemplative expressions.

The Weekend

My weekends weren't exactly exciting with me not having any friends, as my stint in the Jefferson Centre had made sure that all of them had abandoned me once they heard about me and the dreaded MI, or mental illness.

They had all scarpered faster than a group of souls who had suddenly found an escape from the excruciatingly painful torment of the bowels of Hell.

So, what was I to do with myself? It was too early to start going out with people from work yet as they tended to be secretive about their private lives and only let out small snippets of information about **themselves, and I didn't feel confident enough to go** out anywhere on my own.

So I had started a new hobby: neuro-linguistic programming, or NLP.

I had bought several CDs and books off the internet from one person in particular and was very surprised when, one day after listening to several CDs, I received an email from him.

It read:

Zahid,
I have an invitation here from a dear brother,
follow the link below and see if we are for you.
Warmly,
Igor Jones

I followed the link and realised it was asking me to join a secret society, the secret order of the 'Gods of the Dark Moon'.

I was really perplexed — why would anyone want me to join them? I wasn't rich, I wasn't famous, I wasn't anything special at all, in fact I thought I was a bit below par. So why?

There was a contract which had to be printed out and signed, but the more I read the more wary I became. It was asking me to sign a blood oath to 'the God of the Dark Moon'.

There was no way I was going to sign a blood oath to anyone, let alone the God of the Dark Moon, whoever he may be.

I switched off my computer and realised I would have to think twice about ordering any more CDs from Igor Jones as those hypnosis CDs could be hypnotizing me to do anything.

Even then, I thought my behaviour at times was a bit odd and I now see that it all started from the point when I had first started listening to the CDs about a year ago, about the same time that I thought the principalities of Hell were vying for my soul.

That's it! No more hypnosis CDs for me...

I fixed myself something to eat: jacket potato, cheese and beans and a nice glass of cold milk.

Nothing fancy, but then I wasn't a very good cook, as could be attested by the fact I tended to eat the same type of food day in and day out.

With little to do, I simply lay back, listened to music and thought about Natalie and how beautiful she was, so caring and compassionate. I have to admit it, it was a real turn on and I was slowly beginning to forget about Jenni and think more and more about Natalie.

Did she have a boyfriend? I had never got around to asking her but was determined to find out.

I let my thoughts wander as I lay on my bed listening to music and thinking about Natalie, and how nice it would be if I could only be with her now... I drifted off to sleep.

The Third Week

Things had gone from bad to worse very quickly.

Almost every day that week we had an incident with a patient. It seemed perverse, and unfair of me to think it, but it was as if they were each taking it in turns to have a go at the staff. When one of the patients had done their best the day before, they would then calm down and another patient would start in their place.

It was coming to the end of the week and the only person who had kept a low profile and not kicked off in some way so far was Christopher Haunton, so we were all expecting it but it was still a surprise when it came.

Christopher had spent most of the week staying in **his room. I still hadn't cracked his hard veneer but I** thought I was making slow but steady progress, and **then it happened…**

I was sitting in the day room not watching the television but instead listening carefully to a patient when the alarm sounded. I got up and ran into the corridor.

I saw Christopher punch Leon and Trisha grab his arm; Natalie grabbed his other arm and Leon tried to force him down to the ground, but he was too strong and punched upward, like a man possessed. By this time I had reached them and stood not knowing what to do but all the time wanting to protect my teammates.

Christopher grabbed Natalie by her long blond hair and she screamed as he threw her across the floor.

That's it!

I dived in and grabbed one of his arms, Leon another arm and Trisha put her ample weight onto his back. We forced him down the corridor and into the robust room.

Once in the robust room things seemed to change; the dim light and lack of sound seemed to settle Christopher somewhat.

"Let go of me!"

"Not until you've calmed down," said Leon, a bruise appearing on his face just above his scar.

"OK. OK," he said, more subdued.

We let go of him and he fell face first onto the mat. He got up again and faced us, his back against the wall like some caged animal.

Just then Natalie came in looking bloody and bruised around her face, in her hand a small container of water and some tablets.

Leon took them from her.

"Here, take these and you can go to your room."

"No, I am not taking any fucking tablets!"

Christopher launched at Leon and hit him in the head again. The tablets and water went flying over the floor. Leon, being taller, used both hands to try and get a hold of him but we could all see it wasn't going to be enough. We all dived on Christopher and pinned him to the mat on the floor.

Leon and Trisha held him down while I sat on his legs. Natalie came back a few minutes later with an injection in her hands.

"Pull his trousers down," said Leon.

Hearing this Christopher started to struggle even more, and screamed "You bastards!"

It was no use, he was too tightly held down. I managed to pull his trousers down after fiddling with his belt and Natalie injected his behind.

The alarms were still sounding and now we heard other staff running down the corridor. Two large males in white shirts, black ties and black trousers entered the room.

"Go turn it off," said Leon. "We will be okay in here now. Go and take care of the other patients."

I realised that it had taken all of about three minutes. As I left I looked back and heard Leon say something I'd heard him say before, which puzzled me again and had been doing so for some time now.

"It wasn't him."

One of the other guys just nodded.

What the hell do they mean? And who is supposed to be 'him'? It's beginning to drive me round the twist. If I'm not careful I will end up in here as a patient. I'm going to have to listen more carefully to people's conversations to find out exactly what is going on.

I turned off the alarm, exited the office and saw Natalie walking down the corridor in her blue nurse's uniform. Her face was pinched and taut, she had a red bruise on the side of her face where she had hit the wall and a drop of blood on the shoulder of her uniform. Her hair however was neatly combed.

She must have just combed it in the staff room, which was little more than a toilet and a few hooks to hang your coats on.

"That wanker's just gone and given me a nasty bruise, it really hurts."

"Yeah it looks painful, do you want a drink?"

"Yeah, coffee no sugar please…" She paused, looked at me and smiled. "You did really well back then, thanks for helping out."

I smiled back.

"I just did what I could."

I was on the verge of asking her, I really wanted to ask her then if she had a boyfriend. But before I could — maybe I paused just a little too long, she said:

"I better go do an incident form," and was gone.

I went to the ADL kitchen to make myself and Natalie a drink. I knew Leon and the other staff members wouldn't want one because they were still tied up with Christopher and were likely to be for about the next two hours, or until he calmed down.

He calmed down after an hour. At about 7:20pm he went to his room where he stayed for the rest of the shift.

When I eventually got in, I switched on my computer and noticed I had received an email from the group calling themselves the Gods of the Dark Moon.

As I read through it I couldn't help but feel something was wrong. Very wrong indeed.

It started as a small niggle in the back of my mind and then grew and grew until I knew without doubt that I was being watched. I felt an evil suffocating power behind me in my bedroom looking down on me and my leg had started to throb again with a deep and evil pain.

I felt so scared that I didn't dare turn around and look, so scared that my fingers were trembling. I don't know how long I sat like that, in the presence of the strange negative entity, it could have been a few minutes or a few hours.

I eventually realised that a cramp had set in both of the lower parts of my legs as I had a habit of sitting on the chair with my feet on it, with one knee up and one facing down.

I can't tell you how relieved I felt when eventually the power behind me seemed to diminish. I crawled over to my bed and lay still.

The Nightmare

It was night, a large full moon hung solitarily in the soulless empty night.

The chilly wind blew against my skin sending goose bumps up my arms. I stretched and arched my back taking it all in.

There was no sound apart from the wind. I could smell the deep earthy smell of something but I knew not what it was, like soil mixed with something alive, something pungent which hurt my nose.

I looked into the distance and saw something moving, something small and far away. It chilled me to the core, freezing me to the spot and making the blood rush through my veins and pump into my ears.

My breath came in short gasps as I realised what I was looking at. I knew without doubt that one of the princes of the principalities of Hell was here, which **one I couldn't be sure, but as I looked at the thing in** the distance a sound came to me over the wind, a sound which sent shivers running through my soul like the stabs of a cold knife against soft warm flesh.

Sssshhh!! The hiss of a snake, alive and deadly. Sssshhhhh!! The snake got bigger and bigger and I could see it now in the bright moonlight as it came closer, like a train which had left its tracks and come alive with a deep evil energy.

It was less than twenty metres away now, it reared up, towering over me. Large slit eyes glared malevolently down on me. I started to shake, adrenalin now coursing through my veins.

The snake opened its mouth and a black forked tongue and two long sharp needle-like teeth stared back at me. Copious globules of poison dripped from its jaws, causing the concrete on which it landed to sizzle and melt.

Ssshhhhhh! It hissed again, eyeing me with a deep hunger. It lunged. I turned and fled.

I ran past the houses on the right and left with sightless windows which stared at my horror but were unable to give me any solace or comfort.

I ran past the tall, now dead, lampposts whose beautiful warm light failed to bathe my skin or light my way in the inky blackness which surrounded me like a leech, draining all strength and warmth from my body.

I ran and the snake followed behind me, hissing, always there, always hissing. Sweat dripped from my brow, my feet became sore from the tireless exertion **as I desperately tried to escape. I saw the snake's shadow looming over me…**

Utterly exhausted, I knew that this could only be a dream, real snakes **weren't twenty feet tall, nor did** they suck all your strength from you, my mind started to tick.

If this is a dream then I can do anything… I thought for a second and concentrated.

Suddenly there were two of me running. I looked at my other self, not a drop of sweat on his brow and no indication that he was stressed; as I looked at him I got the impression that here was someone who was just out for a short morning stroll.

He winked at me, smiled, and relief flooded through me like whisky intoxicating my body and giving it new strength.

I knew what he was going to do and then he did it; he sprinted to the left and I to the right. I looked over my shoulder and relaxed slightly, thinking I would **now be free from the snake as it wouldn't know who to go after. And then the unthinkable happened...**

I felt like shards of ice had been sprayed through my soul. The snake! Oh my god!

The snake seemed to metamorphose; suddenly where there had been one snake, now there were two. **Instead of halving my problem I'd doubled it.** Dread descended on me then, a deep kind of eternal dread which went to the core of my being and chipped away at my resolve.

I couldn't run any further, I had run and run and now it was just too much. My pace slowed and then I saw it, like a beacon of light on a cold bleak night. The arch! If only I could make it to the giant marble arch in the distance.

My legs found new strength and I sprinted even faster, now leaving the shadow of the looming snake behind me. It hissed.

Sssssshhhhh!

I made it to the arch and I felt the snake stop behind me, unable to penetrate the arch. My feet slowed, sweat dripped down my clothing, I bent over double in excruciating pain and hope surged through me again as I knew I had beaten the snake.

Its name came to me then — not a snake but a demon — Leviathan.

As my breathing returned to normal and the pain in my chest lessened, I heard a distant rumbling. Unsure what it was I stood stock-still listening to it.

Then the ground under me started to shake. I wobbled unable to keep my balance. The ground erupted and I was caught in the jaws of Leviathan. It closed its mouth.

Arrrgggghhh!!

I awoke covered in sweat and trembling with fear.

The light was still on but the flat was silent as a grave. I listened intently to each and every sound.

Nothing.

I closed my eyes and tried to gather myself: a nightmare, that was all it had been. Just a nightmare, I said to myself, trying to find new strength where I felt none, and slowly I passed out into a dreamless sleep.

The Anti-Christ

The next few days at work were much quieter; the patients seemed to settle and relax into themselves more and left most of the staff alone.

It was just after 6:30pm and I was waiting to go on my break. I stood in the doorway of the dayroom trying to listen to Natalie's and Leon's conversation.

I heard only a few words as the noise from the television kept interrupting my concentration and hearing, but then I heard something which puzzled me.

"He's here," said Leon.
"What?" asked Natalie.
"The capstone has been put on…"

The noise of the TV blocked out the rest. The news was on the TV; the story was about the capstone being put onto the great pyramid in Egypt, as if it was such a big deal. Why were so many people bothered about the pyramids? To me they were just huge lumps of rock in the middle of another huge lump of wasteland.

Then I heard…
"Antichrist on Earth."

This really shocked me.

What is this all about? What do the pyramids have to do with the Antichrist being on Earth?

"The prophecy in the Dead Sea Scrolls is coming true," continued Leon.

"Holy shit! That means Lucifer's time on Earth is drawing near."

"It's closer than we thought. Even now the demons are gathering. I can sense them at night above our city waiting to come down."

"The murder rate according to the police has almost doubled in this city in the last two months alone. The demons are making their play, they are possessing those who have been 'opened' and controlling them and…" Leon went quiet, not finishing the sentence. His voice had a soft faraway feel to it.

"…and making them do unspeakable things," finished Natalie.

Demons don't exist. Lucifer doesn't exist, that's all mumbo jumbo, I thought angrily.

What the hell are these people on? They shouldn't be running a psychiatric hospital, they should be in one!

"I think they will be looking for a way into our patients. I am worried about Zahid." Leon paused, "I think he's the weak link in the chain here."

"I do too. He doesn't pray or have any faith. He will make an easy target for Lucifer and his demons," said Natalie in a whisper which I could barely hear.

"I heard what the staff at the Jefferson Centre said about him; it was Leviathan that was after him. I fear for his soul. We've got to do something to help him."

"We can't." Leon sounded angry and worn out now. "Not until we have the go-ahead from those upstairs."

"I know, it's really frightening. We're watching, sitting idly by, while he has to defend himself against the minions of Hell. And the worst of it is that he doesn't even know what he's got himself into."

"He should leave before the Gods of the Dark Moon find out he's working here. We should try to make him leave," said Leon.

What was all this about, wanting me out of my job, which I had just started a few weeks ago? Were they racists and if not what the hell did the Gods of the Dark Moon have to do with all this?

"Oh my God!" exclaimed Natalie. "If the prophecy of the capstone is true then the whole world is in deep trouble and Zahid is the least of our problems…"

"We can't have him working here in his present state of ignorance, he's a liability," finished Leon.

Before I could stop myself I'd stepped into the conference room but before I could speak Natalie's expression silenced me. She was white as a ghost and her delicate fingers which held a fork in her hands were trembling.

They both looked up at me then, realising that I must have been listening.

"What's all this about Lucifer and demons?" I asked.

Their expressions darkened and the look they gave me made me feel fear in my stomach. I felt gutted that these people I had come to like and rely on would cast me out now and not tell me what was happening, but their faces were fixed and I knew there was no way that I was going to get anything other than a shouting match out of them, so I swallowed all my emotions and said:

"It doesn't matter, I'm not really interested. Do you want a drink of tea or coffee?"

"No," they both said loudly and in unison, and I took the opportunity to excuse myself.

For the rest of the shift I was in the doghouse. None of the staff would talk to me properly and only gave me short instructions when they needed to. My heart had sunk when Natalie had gone from a caring compassionate person I could trust to a mean **callous nurse who didn't care about me or how I felt,** but that was how they were for the rest of the shift. It hurt deep inside.

A few days later something happened to me that made me feel very uncomfortable. I needed to talk to **someone about it but couldn't with them all being** mean sods against me, though Natalie could tell something was up; her hardness, I noticed, was mellowing a bit. I was just walking up the corridor when she called me over.

"Zahid, come in here," she said, indicating the conference room. We entered and she switched on the light.

"What's up?" I asked, slightly confused.

"You. What's troubling you? And how did you get that nasty dent in your car?" she asked.

I took a deep breath…

The Gods of the Dark Moon

It was the 4th of October and the weather was not really that bad but bad enough to make you want to be in out of the cold.

I was out shopping at my local grocery store and although I didn't like to admit it, I had used my car to get there even though it was only a ten-minute walk away.

In the medium-sized supermarket I noticed something odd, there was a man in black trousers and black leather jacket always behind me. I turned left in an aisle, he turned left; I turned right, and he turned right. I walked into the female toiletries area; he walked into the female toiletries area.

I turned around and he stood there staring at me barely two feet away. Black lank hair, pale drawn face, black sunglasses, smooth black leather jacket, black trousers and shiny shoes.

Is this a friend of Christopher's?

He held out his hand in a pleasant manner. I didn't take it. There was a long cold silence.

"We are the Gods of the Dark Moon," he said, just loud enough to be heard by me but no one else.

"What do you want with me? I've told you I want no part in your cult."

"We could make things worthwhile for you, very worthwhile," he said, taking off his sunglasses. His eyes were as blue as marble.

"We need someone on the inside."
"What? On the inside of what?"
"What do you do?"
"I'm a healthcare support worker."
"We know."
"Look, you freak! Just leave me the fuck alone!"

Suddenly some of the other shoppers looked at us, but the man in black wasn't fazed. He just stood there implacably, like a mannequin in a shop.

"I'm disappointed."

Could that have been real? No way! His eyes have just changed colour from blue to emerald green.

"I thought we could have worked well together."

I just stared at him, showing him that I wouldn't be intimidated.

"Your turn will come soon, unless you reconsider. Let this be a warning to you," he said simply and walked away.

What does that mean? It sounds like a threat!

After paying for my groceries I left in an anxious state. As I exited the store I walked a little too quickly and looked around to see if anyone was watching me but there was no one there. The man in the black leather jacket had disappeared.

My breath condensed into water vapour in front of me and the cold sent a chill through my bones. The sunlight was bright and harsh and hurt my eyes. The pavement was dangerous with sleet underfoot and I nearly slipped several times as I carried my groceries back to my car. My red Ford Ka, white with frost,

was not really a man's car I know but it was the only car that had been within my budget and that I liked.

I placed the groceries in the passenger seat and strapped on my seatbelt. I took another look around. I saw a man dressed in a thick coat and a scarf, he paid me little attention and was gone in a few seconds.

There were some children playing with their football against a wall. I heard its dull thud as it rebounded off the wall, the sound sending fear running through my veins.

Why? I don't know.

I started the car and was gone from that place and the strange man in the black leather jacket. I put some music on and relaxed. As I drove I let all fear leave me and started to think about Natalie again.

Her soft face...her tender smile...her concerned eyebrows...her glossy hair...a white van!

"Arrggh!" I screamed as I suddenly swerved the car, half not believing what was happening.

I felt a burning pain in my leg as the car shook with the force of the blow. A van had come out of a side street at speed and hit me on the side, sending me into the opposing lane of traffic.

My life flashed before me and I thought this was it. I saw my primary school teacher looking at me through his thick-rimmed glasses. *"Life's not fair,"* **he'd said and anger welled deep within my stomach.**

Life might not be fair but I'm not going without a fight.

I swerved the car out of the way of the oncoming traffic and back onto my side of the road. My car spun and I stamped on the brakes; the car went up the pavement and came to a stop.

The white van disappeared into the distance as fast as it had come. I sat breathlessly trying to catch my breath.

Horrible pain ran up and down my left leg and I could feel that my lips were wet. In the rear-view mirror I noticed my lips were red with blood; I had bitten my lip in fear and now blood dribbled down my chin onto my blue designer jacket.

"Shit!" I said wiping my chin. "Bastards!" I said more loudly, hitting the steering wheel with my hand which I instantly regretted as pain lanced up my arm.

I got out inspecting the damage. The damage was mainly towards the rear side of the body; the car was still drivable. I called the police on my mobile.

Natalie listened patiently and when I had finally recounted my story she took a deep breath.

"Okay, Zahid," she smiled nervously, "I need to speak with Leon and I promise I will get back to you as soon as I can."

She exited the room and I noticed how pert her arse looked in her blue uniform.

Oh Natalie... if only...

Near the end of the shift, Natalie walked up to me and said:

"I've had a word with Leon about you; we're going to discuss you in the ward meeting on Wednesday and take it from there."

"Oh great, why aren't I invited to the ward meeting?" For an instant she looked totally drained and exhausted and then the caring pleasant smile was back.

Then she said something which shocked me to my core.

"I'm only saying this because I like you."

She smoothed the left arm of her nurse's uniform with her right hand, a habit I had seen her do often when she was nervous, and continued:

"You should find another job as soon as you can."

"What are you talking about?" I asked, slightly taken aback.

"Working here is very dangerous. You don't know what you're getting yourself into."

But before I could ask anything else, Leon entered the office and Natalie moved away, letting me know the conversation was over.

I was off work on Wednesday, the day of the meeting.

No doubt they had arranged it like that so I wouldn't know what had been discussed. I lay in my one-bedroom flat, face down on my bed and thinking about my life.

What has become of me? When I was young I showed so much promise but somewhere along the line, I've lost my way.

Soft gentle tears flowed down my face into my pillow as I cried.

What am I crying for? I'm not sure… I just want a girlfriend so badly — no, not any girlfriend but Natalie… only Natalie. But she hardly notices me. I thought about her soft face… her tender smile… her concerned eyebrows… her glossy hair… Oh Natalie.

I closed my eyes and cried in anguish, feeling the pain deep inside my heart. I thought about my primary school teacher again then. His words, which had been said to me at the tender age of nine, came back to me now, mocking me, haunting me and savagely twisting a knife deep within my heart.

Life's not fair, Zahid… Life's not fair… The words echoed inside my head round and round.

What would they decide today? Would they let me into their close-knit network? I pray they will, and if they do, that means I will be one step closer to understanding all of what is going on… and… one step closer to getting Natalie.

I felt stultified in that flat; all I ever did was to lie on my bed in that flat.

I want to go for a drive, get some fresh air, get out of this damn shithole of a flat and my life but I daren't — what if that weird cult, the Gods of the Dark Moon are about again. No, it's too dangerous… I daren't risk it.

So I was stuck once again, like so often in my life. *Stuck…*

The Hospital Network

The next day when I arrived for work, everything felt different; the early shift staff were much friendlier towards me as I arrived.

I began to think maybe the decision had gone in my favour.

I arrived on the late shift just before 1.30pm, put my jacket away in the staff room and made my way and sat down in the conference room, waiting for the others to arrive for handover. I looked at my watch: I was early by about fifteen minutes.

After a few minutes Natalie entered.

"Hi Zahid," she said with a wide smile and I smiled back.

"Hi Natalie…How are you?"

"I'm fine. I've got some good news – we came to a decision about you and Leon said it would be okay if I told you."

I sat up listening eagerly and could almost feel my ears standing on end.

"Yes?" I queried.

"We're going to let you into the hospital network. After you told us what's happened, we've got no choice now".

"Great!" I said, unable to hide my excitement.

"We're not having handover today, it's just you and me as I fill you in on what this place is about."

"Okay, I'm listening."

"Have you noticed how all the wards are shaped like crucifixes and how we have people brought in from all over the country?"

"Yes, I had noticed that."

"Well, the people we bring in are demon-possessed or in danger of being possessed. I know this sounds unbelievable right now but keep listening and it will all make sense."

"OK."

"A lot of them have dabbled in the occult at one time or another and opened themselves up to dark forces, either by doing Ouija boards or dark spells."

"What, magic exists?" I asked, half disbelieving what I was hearing.

"Magic is real, very real. As real as you and me sitting here now."

She took a deep breath, pausing, and I saw her eyes seemed distant as if she was thinking about something.

"It usually starts off by people wanting to speak to a recently dead relative that they miss, or a love spell, and then it slowly escalates until they are performing more and more powerful spells. Not everyone is opened up to dark forces by magic; some practise self-hypnosis, which is just magic by another name."

At this I had a sharp intake of breath and she looked at me.

"Why, what's wrong?"

"I've been practising self-hypnosis on myself and was contacted by that strange cult."

"We know. Once they contacted you, we had no choice but to let you in."

"I've got one question: why was I given the job when you had so many people to choose from? I mean you must have known about my schizophrenia."

"We did. We gave you the job because you are sensitive."

"What do you mean?"

"You're sensitive to psychic phenomena. Have you ever noticed any part of your body start to hurt when the alarms go off?"

"Yeah, I have noticed that, what's that all about?"

"When Lucifer tries to possess one of our patients, the alarms go off. And we feel his evil in our bodies. That's why the paint is thicker — to keep out all types of negative energy. You must have noticed by now that the patients are originally agitated when brought in by police, but after being in here a few minutes they tend to calm down." She absent-mindedly began to stroke her left arm with her right hand. "That's due to the paint."

I sat amazed by all that I was hearing. I knew something strange was going on at the hospital but I had never in my wildest dreams expected this.

"Wow! No way!" I exclaimed.

Natalie just looked at me and smiled, a smile that melted my heart. I felt so happy then just sitting next to her, with each other as our only company.

I love you. I wanted to say it. *I really love you Natalie.*

I began to say it but the words got stuck in my throat. I coughed instead. She ignored my coughing and carried on, that faraway look in her eyes.

"Have you read the Bible?"

"I've read bits of it."

"You should read it, I will give you one before you finish work today. I brought one in with me. You see, there was a war in Heaven. Lucifer, who was supposed to be really good-looking, rebelled against God. He was jealous of God and wanted to take his place on the throne and rule all of creation. So God cast him and the rebellious angels out of Heaven and he landed here on Earth. He gave men power and magic in return for their service to him and he built up a network, but you may know them better as the cult of the Gods of the Dark Moon. They are very **dangerous people."**

I gasped. I knew they had something to do with this but I had never realised that they worshipped Satan himself. I could feel my heartbeat in my own ears, pumping like a giant drum. I felt the colour drain from my face.

"You don't look too good," she said staring straight at me. "You've gone white. Wait here, I will get you some water."

She exited the room and was back in a few seconds with a cup of water. I drank it thirstily and set it back down on the table.

"Better?" she said.

"Better. Thanks," I replied and she continued.

"The war between good and evil has been going on for thousands of years unseen by most people, or 'sheeple' as the Dark Moon like to call them. We are the only thing standing in their way of bringing Lucifer to Earth and their total world domination. Recently in Egypt, the capstone has been put on; this signifies the arrival of the Antichrist on Earth. At the minute, we think he is just another force released from Hell but his demons have grown stronger and now attack us every day.

"Last Wednesday when you were off, we called in a priest from the Vatican and had this whole place exorcised. It's helped in reducing some of the attacks but the demons are gaining in strength, and I fear for our patients and the world outside."

"Holy shit! The Antichrist – now you are really freaking me out."

"Don't worry, God will protect us."

"I hope you're right Natalie, right now I feel like a duck in a turkey shoot."

Natalie burst out laughing. "You really have a way of describing things," she said, tapping me gently on my arm with her hand.

Right then I stretched out my hand and grabbed hers in mine.

"Natalie…" We stared at each other, eyes wide and faces beaming.

"Natalie, there is something I want to ask you."

"Yes, go ahead," she said with a small laugh.

"Natalie, I was wondering if you'd like to meet me after work sometime?" Her eyes narrowed and the smile left her face.

"Like on a date?" she said, slightly louder than I thought she should have and right then all my courage and happiness and hope deserted me.

"Yes. Like on a date." My voice sounded weak and the moisture welled up in my eyes which were now on the verge of tears.

Suddenly she burst out laughing.

"I got you then!" she exclaimed.

"What?"

"Yes, I'd love to Zahid!"

She leaned forward and hugged me. I closed my eyes, savouring the moment, wanting to commit it to memory forever...

The Date

It was Saturday October 7th. I had just showered, shaved and been to the toilet and was now putting on my smartest casual clothes, clothes which I had bought for just this occasion. A smart black shirt and faded dark black jeans.

I sprayed myself with aftershave and deodorant, even pulling my jeans forward and spraying my **underpants in case I got lucky, which I wasn't expecting to… but there was always hope.**

I slipped on my jacket and rang Natalie as I stared at myself in the mirror. I had just gelled my hair which was cropped short. I heard the ringing tone and waited anxiously holding my breath.

Suddenly I breathed out as silently as I could as I heard:

"Hello, Zahid. I just spent the last hour getting ready and will meet you by Angelo's Pizza Hut in fifteen minutes."

"Natalie, I'm just about to get into my car," I said, gazing at how bulky my chest looked with my jacket on in the mirror. "I will see you in fifteen minutes, hon." I heard a low laugh that was cut short.

"See you in fifteen."

As I walked out to my car my head was spinning. *A whole hour! Wow, she must really like me.*

I felt so happy and now all I had to do was play it cool. No rambling on about inconsequential things, no staring at tits, and definitely no looking at other women. I had found that in the past to be a definite no-no.

Within a few minutes I had arrived at the meeting **place and waited outside Angelo's Pizza Hut in the** dark early night and cold frosty weather.

It was at times like this that sometimes I would wish that I smoked — to make me look cooler, but I **didn't, so I just put my hands in my pockets to keep** them warm. I looked momentarily up at the inky black sky and saw a large full moon hanging strongly in the weak night-time sky. I looked away again quickly.

Not now, now is not the time to get worried about that bunch of freaks.

And then I saw her. She was wearing a smart black dress, and was coming towards me still from some ten metres away. Her walk was pleasant and calm, her hair worn long. I saw her pale beautiful arms glowing under the light of the lamppost and then she was standing in front of me. I took a deep breath and smiled, whilst looking into her deep blue eyes. She smiled back.

Bliss...

The seconds stretched out...

"Zahid," she said touching me on my arm. "Let's get inside, it's too cold out here."

We entered Angelo's pizza restaurant. We waited a few seconds then a waitress saw us and came up to us.

"Do you have anywhere in particular that you would like to sit?" she asked.

I looked around and saw that it wasn't too busy and anywhere looked just fine to me. Natalie just nodded.

"Nowhere in particular," she said.

The waitress smiled and said, "Follow me." She showed us to a comfortable looking table for two in the corner and we both sat down.

I was nervous. I couldn't help it.

Natalie looks so stunning, I can't believe she is here on a date with me.

Natalie smiled again. My throat was parched and I didn't know what to say.

"You've gone quiet Zahid… Say something."

"What do you want me to say?" I said, opening the menu and putting it on the table as a barrier between us.

The smile left her face.

I flattened the menu and stretched out my hand, meaning to touch her hand across the table, but something stopped me halfway. Fear? Insecurity? Self-doubt? All these monsters now reared their ugly heads. Instead of touching her hand and telling her how much I loved and thought of her and how much I'd waited for this moment and wanted to be with her, I just looked down.

"What should we order?" I could hear the sound of disappointment in her voice.

I gazed at the menu quickly, made my choice and told her we should share one big pizza and she agreed. A few moments later a waiter came over and we gave our orders.

We talked quietly making pleasant conversation but my seducing skills, I now realised, left a lot to be desired.

"I really like working on Ward Four, I'm just getting to know the staff and feel really happy that they've let me into their network."

"Yeah, I'm glad you're there, you're really good at your job. You have a good way with the patients and they seem to like you."

"Thanks," I beamed back. "That means a lot to me".

Then there was the dreaded silence that I always seemed to notice hanging around me on first dates.

What do I say next...?

The silence stretched out. My eyes flitted around the restaurant scanning the other occupants. I saw some of them look away, were they looking at me? It felt like it. My bladder suddenly felt tight and I hastily excused myself to Natalie's disappointment. She just looked down and away, and I headed towards the toilet.

The gents were empty. I looked in the mirror, "What the hell are you doing?" I said to myself. "Natalie is so beautiful, and you're making a fool of yourself..." I stared at the reflection of my face which was taut and red; I wiped my face with my hands. "Get a grip."

Suddenly I heard a toilet flush, a man in a jumper and trousers exited the cubicle and smiled.

"Out on a date?" he asked. My face darkened and I stormed out. As I sat back down Natalie looked up at me uncertainly.

Just then the waiter arrived and placed the pizza down. We ate in silence, Natalie looking more and more uncertain all the time and me looking more and more paranoid.

That jerk in the gents; was he working for them?

As we were eating I looked up and saw him leaving with his girlfriend. He smiled and winked. My fist slammed down on the table, startling Natalie and the other occupants nearby.

I thought that was the beginning of the end of any positive opinion Natalie might have had of me. And then it started, her nursing training kicking in; it felt nice and comfortable but left me feeling somewhat lousy and upset.

"What meds are you on Zahid?" she asked, looking down at the pizza as she stroked her right arm with her left hand.

"Risperidone; I've been on most of the meds going."

And then I quickly listed them to show there was nothing wrong with me and I still had enough faculties to know what I was taking: "Olanzapine,

Quetiapine, Clozapine, Mirtazapine, Haldol, and now Risperidone."

She stopped stroking her arm and started to eat the pizza again as I talked.

"What dose of Risperidone?"
"6 milligrams."
"Do you take it night or morning?"
"Half in the morning and half at night."

The pizza seemed to be vanishing faster and faster as we talked.

"How do you find it suits you?"
"It's okay, makes me tired at night and helps me get to sleep but in the morning it can make me feel drowsy."

Natalie went quiet for a second. My eyes flitted around the restaurant again and she caught me doing it.

"I don't think the Gods of the Dark Moon will bother us tonight. It's one of their black Sabbaths so you can stop looking around if you like. And with regard to your medication, maybe… you should increase the dosage or ask your psychiatrist to recommend something else."

My heart sank and my eyes focused squarely on Natalie. I wanted to believe what she said about the Gods of the Dark Moon but my body wouldn't let me, it wouldn't let me relax and what she just said to me about my medication meant she thought I was unwell.

Too unwell to go out with? Probably…

The pizza was all gone.

She looked straight at me and now there was no softness in her voice.

"I don't think we should order a dessert."

"Right."

She got up. "I'm just going to the ladies' and then I think we should go. I'm tired."

I watched her firm arse as she walked quickly away in her black dress. The waitress came and cleared away the plates, and another waiter brought the bill over. I paid half then waited for Natalie to return. When she did, she seemed sad and part of her mascara was slightly smudged. She paid the other half of the bill.

"I think we should go, I've had enough," she said.

"Right," I said with a heavy heart, hating myself for the fact that I had messed it up big time with her.

We said our goodbyes outside and then I was all alone again. I got into my car and drove home in silence.

The Dream

I dreamt. I was sitting on a pier on a dark cold night but didn't feel cold. The person next to me radiated heat and a light glow of sunshine which spread out all around us.

I stared out at the soft calm sea. The waves lapping the shore lazily, I felt bliss, not the kind of bliss felt on a warm summer's morning but a different kind of bliss, the kind felt in one's later years when looking back on an achievement to be immensely proud of, or the kind of bliss felt from the attainment and satisfaction of one's first true love.

Natalie sat next to me, her long blond hair blowing freely in the warm summer breeze. The moon was bright and full but I felt no fear or dread, just a contentment which I had never felt before. The kind of contentment felt after a long lovemaking session, but we had not made love, there was no need for us to, we were content simply to be sitting side by side on this magical supernatural night and at peace.

I saw Natalie turn and face me, she looked at me then with her wide round blue eyes and I saw happiness and I knew that that was also what she saw in mine. She lifted her arm and stretched out her hand, touching mine. The warmth was pure heaven, the touch so powerful and warm.

I didn't want to break the beauty of the moment with my voice so I didn't speak but it was as if she knew what I wanted to say. I heard her voice in my head.

I love you Zahid...

There, she had said what I had wanted to hear for so long.

I will never leave you Zahid, you are my destiny, now and forever.

Tears of joy wanted to come to my eyes but I fought them until the feeling passed.

And I yours Natalie...

She smiled, revealing well-shaped clean white teeth and my heart cried out for this moment to last forever. I returned her smile, her soft hand on top of mine in the bright soft glow of the moon and the sound from the lazy waves. I watched the waves endlessly lapping the shore, our feet dangling freely in the wind... and then I felt it.

The moon was suddenly obscured by a cloud and the night was surrounded in pitch blackness. I felt her hand vanish in the darkness, and then the cloud was gone in a heartbeat. Natalie's warm hand vanished from mine and I looked and knew before I had that she was gone.

I looked around frantically feeling discomfort rush through my body. I saw the waves lapping harder and harder getting higher and higher and more aggressive.

I got up looking all around for Natalie. The night was now shrouded in a darkness I hadn't seen whilst Natalie was there. The darkness encompassed me, I felt it all around me, bearing down on me and trying to expunge me from existence.

Suddenly I saw a faint shimmer of light and a beautiful white hand emerge from the murky water; without thinking I dived in.

I found myself spinning and falling, there was no time here, white light surrounded me and then everything around me started to take shape.

I was on a path about two metres wide; it was a hot **summer's evening and in the distance over the** horizon I could see the red glow of the spectral sun, just about to go down. Trees lined the path on both sides; I looked at them, thin and tall. The trunks were made out of glass with a covering of a crystal canopy at the top, which seemed to capture the light in a way I had never seen before.

The light was held in the foliage of the canopy and glowed redly, giving out light. The trunks were a marvel and shone whitely, reflecting the light from the dying sun.

I started to walk along the path, towards a building I could see in the distance, the sun behind me. The trees stayed with me as they were spread out about every two metres.

I walked and walked. Searching for Natalie...my Natalie. The building in the distance grew closer and closer. It was dome-shaped with two large towers at either side; it reminded me of a picture I had seen of the Taj Mahal.

My love...don't desert me now.

I knew somehow that when I entered the building Natalie would be there waiting for me. I entered the building which was lit by a large circular sphere of light which hung high above me like a bright wide moon.

I saw Natalie standing at the far end before a dais in a white wedding dress but there was now no glow of light coming from her. Pews stood on either side of me leading up to the dais, but there were no guests for our wedding. I slowly walked towards her holding my breath.

Then I was standing next to Natalie, looking at her veil, wanting so much to lift it and see her face. I raised my arm, meaning to lift it but something stopped me.

If this is our wedding then where is the priest…and then I heard a door open behind the dais and a priest **walk out but his face was blurred to me and I couldn't** make it out.

I looked at Natalie, I was now trembling with anticipation and excitement. I lifted the veil and screamed.

It wasn't Natalie! A lizard's face confronted me, eyes deep green and slit, a forked tongue hissing out at me, the skin scaled and bumpy. I looked up in shock and saw the priest, his face was now visible — the man from the Gods of the Dark Moon I had met in the store. His eyes were slit and green too and he made a hissing noise as his tongue flicked out. I screamed.

"Arrrgr!" I suddenly awoke covered in a sheen of sweat.

My night clothes were clammy and from the light shining from the weak lightbulb I could make out that it was 2am. I got up and went to make myself a cup of tea.

Natalie

It was Monday. I sat in handover just a few minutes after 1:30pm, with Natalie, Leon, Trisha, and Maxine, the latest addition to the team. It seemed the higher-ups had decided having only four staff on at any one time wasn't safe anymore.

"Okay," Leon said, the scar stretching slightly as he spoke, "now that we are all here, I will start."

He looked around quickly and I noticed he and Natalie looked at me then looked away again quickly. Natalie was refusing to meet my gaze; every time I looked at her she looked down or away.

Shit, I messed up big time.

Leon continued:

"The Gods of the Dark Moon had their special winter Sabbath this weekend and we believe they will strike soon. Their power will be strongest around this time of year and then start to fade again with the end of the dying of the sun after December 25th."

I lifted my hand. "Excuse me, what do you mean, 'dying of the sun'?"

"The shortening of the daylight hours increases the strength of the darkness and Lucifer, their dark lord who they get their power from. That means we have to be on our guard until December 25th, after which time some of their power will have dissipated. It's mid-October now so for the next two months we have to be very sharp."

Leon looked around, but nobody met his gaze, their own thoughts being held close to their chests. My own thoughts were on the Antichrist; he was here on Earth as an incarnate force looking for a body to habitate.

That meant their power would only grow until someone put an end to him and that someone would have to be far braver than me or anyone in the room, I thought, but remained silent.

"The higher-ups in management realise what a dangerous time this is for us, so have sanctioned the funding for another member of staff," he said smiling and looking at Maxine. "This is Maxine, for those of you who haven't met her yet. She has been transferred here from another hospital, so I'm sure all you good people will welcome her into our fold."

Maxine smiled and stood up; she was about five feet four with dark ginger hair and blue eye shadow, slimly built but with a hard-worn face which showed it had been through some struggles and tribulations.

"All the staff so far have been really nice, thank you," she said and sat back down.

I saw everybody smile and for a second caught Natalie's gaze but she looked away again.

Shit I am a fool… will she give me another chance or have I blown it for good?

Handover finished and then we exited the office and made our way to the rest of the ward and our main duties. I put the tea and coffee drinks trolley out, and went to the office to get the menus on which I would write the patients' names.

I then sat in the day room, which only held a few patients, and started to write the names on the menus.

Like I often did, I quickly scanned the room trying to get a feel for the mood of the patients, they seemed unconcerned and quietly sat watching TV.

Things didn't seem too bad but I knew all that could change in the blink of an eye, and as if to prove this thought correct I heard a loud scream echoing down the corridor. I got up and went to look and saw Edward walking down the corridor.

Edward was an elderly gentleman, about sixty-five years old, whose main bad behavioural symptoms seemed to consist of stripping off naked and walking down the corridors. His other 'trick', as I liked to call it, was urinating himself and his bed and then struggling with the staff as we tried to clean him up.

He was naked and soaking wet, which I thought was either sweat or water but couldn't be sure from this far away, but at the back of my mind I thought it might even be urine.

As I got close to Edward I realised it was water as there wasn't a stink of urine. He'd opened the tap in his room and stripped off his clothes and soaked himself in water. I pulled my gloves out of my back pockets, put them on and put an arm around Edward.

"Come on Edward, let's go back to your room, get dry and get some clothes on, you can't be running around naked with all these ladies around here can you," and guided him back to his room.

From his expression it was obvious he didn't want to go, but a bit of force, applied as gently as possible, made things easier for me, and Edward had no choice as I guided him more firmly when he tried to struggle.

Once in his bedroom, he refused to get dressed or even help me to get him dressed. So I shut his bedroom door and got a chair and sat outside his bedroom. Then, I heard him start to wail and within a short space of time he tried to come out but I grabbed him around the shoulder and pushed him back into his room.

And that was how the majority of my day was spent; sitting outside an elderly naked person's bedroom and listening to him wailing.

Later on at about 7pm, by which time Edward had tired himself out and fallen asleep, I noticed Patrick was very subdued. He slunk down the corridor to and fro from his room as he normally did but this time without making a sound. I stopped him in the corridor.

"Are you alright Patrick?" I asked.

He just nodded, staring at me with his dark blue baleful eyes.

"Patrick, I said are you alright?" I asked again.

He nodded.

"Zahid, I'm scared."

"What's scaring you?"

"I think something bad is going to happen very soon."

"Okay, Patrick, try not to worry too much about it. Let us, the professionals, deal with things on the ward, okay?"

He nodded again, and then almost inaudibly said:

"Keep an eye on Christopher, he's dangerous," and then he shuffled past me.

I walked down the corridor, turned left and found Christopher's bedroom; he wasn't in there. I then walked back the way I had come and looked in the quiet room; there he was, with the light on low and the Bible in his hand.

Over the last few days I believed I had made some progress in breaking his hard veneer. He had now started to call me by my name and ask me the odd question about God and the Devil and what I thought about good and evil.

I entered the quiet room now.

"Hi, Christopher," I said, noticing the thick blackness outside the window.

He looked up briefly, *still guarded*, I thought.

"Hi Zahid," he said in that deep intelligent voice which seemed so out of place in his dishevelled body.

"Reading the Bible?" I asked, trying to think of something.

"Here," he said suddenly, closing the Bible and handing it to me, "open it on a page at random."

Slightly nervous and not wanting to do anything which might upset Christopher, I did as he asked. I opened the Bible and read the first bit I came to.

"Be self-controlled and alert. Your enemy the Devil prowls around" — at the mention of the Devil, Christopher seemed to tense slightly but I continued, "like a roaring lion looking for someone to devour—"

"Resist him," interrupted Christopher angrily, "standing firm in the faith, because you know that your brothers throughout the world are undergoing the same kind of sufferings."

I just sat silently not knowing what to say.

"And what about my brothers?" asked Christopher angrily and then I took a chance.

I knew it could backfire and blow up in my face but then I said, "Christopher, I am your brother am I not?"

At this he seemed to go rigid and I thought he would launch at me but then he relaxed again and started to laugh. His voice was sadder now.

"You remind me of my mum," he said. "When I was little there was a little Asian kid in my street who none of the other kids would play with, and one day my mother saw him standing in the street on his own just watching us play. Leaving him out." He paused, thoughtfully, his voice lower and sadder, "And my mother came up to me and asked why I wasn't playing with him and I said I didn't know…" He paused.

"My mother told me he was my brother, and we should all play together. When I mentioned this to the other kids they ignored it but I went back to him, and we played with my football. I can still remember the way it thudded against the wall." I saw his eyes held some moisture all of a sudden; were those tears or just water?

"We became best friends and I always thought about my mother and what she had given me that day. A different way of looking at the world, and then as I got older, the bills were piling up, my father had left us and we were struggling to survive." A tear fell from his right eye.

"God abandoned us, me and my mother, who had been so religious and then she did it. She took her own life because she wasn't able to cope. I vowed that day never to be like my mother, never to pray to some weak God who would also abandon me in my hour of need."

More tears flowed down Christopher's face. Wanting to spare him embarrassment and loss of dignity, I handed him a box of tissues from the side-table and left saying:

"Nice talking to you Christopher, talk to you again soon."

Now I was the one that felt bad. I had wanted to get the information out of Christopher and he had given me more than he'd ever given me before but now I felt lousy that I had tried to manipulate him, not caring about his feelings. It seemed I wasn't just learning things about him but also about myself.

I headed to the office and found Natalie and Leon filling in details in the folders. I stood waiting for them to acknowledge me; they looked up.

"Patrick thinks Christopher's going to be the one we need to keep an eye on."

"Yes, we do, too," said Leon.

Natalie piped up. "Only problem is that he's expecting to go home on leave tomorrow, and when we don't allow it, all hell is going to break loose".

"When are you going to tell him?" I asked.

"Tomorrow just after handover while we've got the late and the early staff still on duty," said Leon.

I felt a chill go through me. I knew things were going to get very scary sooner rather than later around here.

I went and sat down in the dayroom 'to observe the patients' but what that really meant was watch TV. I saw Maxine sitting watching a soap and she looked at me and smiled, a warm caring smile. I smiled back. Then I heard Natalie's gentle footsteps enter the ADL kitchen, so I got up and went to the kitchen.

"Natalie…?"

"Yes?" she said softly.

"I made an appointment with my psychiatrist to have a review of my medication," I said.

"That's good then isn't it?"

"Natalie…" I said trying to muster all my courage, "I'm sorry if I acted oddly on Saturday. I was wondering if you would give me another chance?"

Natalie just looked down for a long moment.

"Like another date, you mean?

My voice got stuck in my throat, but I managed to say "Yes, like on another date."

I thought she was going to refuse. I held my breath with anticipation.

"Zahid…I do like you but I don't think we are right for each other."

I felt my heart beating rapidly and anger welled deep within me.

Not right for each other?

"Natalie, please, just give me one more chance."

I knew I was going red.

She looked up at me then into my deep brown eyes with her clear blue eyes which I found so alluring and smiled. I smiled back and suddenly the tension was broken.

"I will think about it," was all she said and she turned away.

I knew the conversation was over. I exited the kitchen, hope welling deep within my heart once again.

The rest of the shift passed off uneventfully. I, along with Maxine, did all the little jobs we needed to do and the patients remained subdued and settled.

Friday

The next day I arrived with some trepidation, not sure what to expect but determined to protect Natalie and the other staff.

I had to admit Natalie was constantly on my mind these days, even to the extent that the Gods of the Dark Moon had taken a back seat, which I knew was dangerous as they had threatened my life already.

I entered the conference room and had handover given to me by one of the early staff, and then we all entered the ward. Leon spoke to everyone just before we exited the conference room.

"I'm going to tell Christopher now, so be prepared for the alarms to go off."

I looked at Natalie and she just smiled at me, making me feel warm and happy.

Maybe...just maybe she has changed her mind.

I saw Leon, Trisha and another large male staff member from the early staff walk up to Christopher who was slowly walking down the corridor. I hung back as the others gave Leon and Christopher some room. I waited for all hell to break loose but was shocked when Leon walked back calmly, and Christopher turned round and quietly walked back down the corridor to the quiet room.

In a way nothing happening was more unnerving **really because I wasn't expecting it, but I knew that**

Christopher was smart. He was probably just biding his time until the early staff went home.

I saw Patrick give Christopher a wide berth as he walked past him. He walked past me without a word, rapidly breathing and wheezing for breath.

Poor Patrick. In a psychiatric hospital for the last forty years for one mistake. On a late Halloween night all those years ago, he had dabbled with a Ouija board which had opened him up to dark forces.

Things settled back down. It wasn't until later, at around six, just after patients' tea-time, when the sun had set some time ago, and the darkness outside was total, that what I expected to happen happened.

"You fucking bastards!" Christopher shouted down the corridor.

Leon, Natalie, Trisha and I all exited the conference room where we were having our tea.

"What's wrong?" asked Leon, not happy about his tea being interrupted. He tended to get grumpy if his routine was interrupted. I looked around but couldn't see Maxine anywhere.

"You bastards!" said Christopher, advancing on us. "Keeping me locked up in here like a caged animal!"

"Look," Leon said calmly, holding out his palms in an open gesture, his six foot two-inch frame equalling that of Christopher's. "No one's keeping you locked up anywhere, we're just looking after you until you're better."

Oh my God! Did I just see that? It seemed to **happen in slow motion and I couldn't believe what I'd seen.** One second Leon was standing talking calmly and the next he crumpled to the floor in slow motion, blood pouring from a wound in his head.

Christopher raised the hammer which he had pulled out from his clothes and tried to hit the semi-conscious Leon again, but Trisha and Natalie ran to him grabbing his arms. I pulled my alarm as the fear ran through me.

The alarm resounded through the ward. I ran to the back of Christopher and tried to push him to the ground but he was too strong, as if he was possessed. He pushed Natalie and Trisha off him and raised the hammer to strike Natalie.

I didn't think about it, I knew I could be in trouble for such a violent action but under the circumstance I believed I had no choice. I kicked Christopher in the groin from behind as hard as I could. He clutched his **balls but didn't go down.**

Natalie ran down the corridor into the robust room.

"He's possessed!" screamed Trisha in her breathy scratchy voice, showing her sharp jagged teeth as she tried to grab his arm which held the hammer, but he dodged backwards and struck her in the face. She collapsed to the floor.

Natalie suddenly emerged from the robust room looking flustered.

"The bottle of holy water is missing!"

Christopher looked at us then; Natalie and I were the only ones stopping him from escaping the ward. He smiled, which chilled me to the core.

His sunglasses had fallen to the floor and his hair was wild and all over the place; he looked like he was demon-possessed and it gave me the shivers.

He sprinted for the main doors.

"It's OK, they are locked," Natalie said, but then the unthinkable happened.

He pushed the doors and they opened.

We stood in shock; how had the doors opened? There was only one way; they had already been opened by someone, but we didn't have time to think about that now.

Then I realised the predicament we were in.

Christopher's aim is to escape and kill someone in a dark rite to increase Lucifer's power over him and over this world.

"We go… got…got to go after him," Natalie shouted over the noise of the alarm, "he means…to kill someone to increase Lucifer's power on this world." She said shakily, "We have… have to stop him."

We gave chase. Just as I exited the main door I saw the door at the far end slam shut. I looked and realised Natalie wasn't with me. I made it to the door at the end of the corridor and ran up the stairs and outside into the dark cold night.

My lungs were suddenly burning but I couldn't let Christopher get away. I saw him by the light of the lamppost casting its hope-filled light into the surrounding blackness.

He ran round a bend in the road and I lost sight of him for a few seconds and then I too rounded the bend. Suddenly a car pulled up from a side road and I saw Christopher trying to get in. I increased my pace and suddenly I was upon him; I punched him hard in the stomach and then kicked him in the groin. He went down, dropping the hammer.

I kicked him hard in the face, and felt something break. He got to his knees and punched me in the stomach; I doubled over. I thrust myself at him as he tried to rise and we both went sprawling into the road, kicks and punches flying.

Something struck me in the head and more blows landed on my back and arm but I held on to him. I returned the blows but my arms were weak and had no strength. I had no energy left and blood poured from a cut to my cheek.

He stood over me, the bright moon hanging like an omen of doom behind him.

"Come on, get in the car!" a woman's voice shouted; a voice I recognised.

Maxine's voice!

He moved away and then came back a few moments later with the hammer in his hands. He raised it to strike. Suddenly I saw something flash from the side and I heard Christopher scream. It was Natalie!

I got up and saw a needle sticking out of Christopher's arse as he turned on Natalie.

"You bitch!" Maxine screamed, getting out of her car.

I jumped on Christopher from behind and punched him in the head. Maxine was suddenly on Natalie.

"Oi!" I heard shouting from some way off and realised Leon was running towards us as fast as he could. Christopher, seeing Leon, tried to get Natalie and Maxine separated. I ran to the car and pulled out the key from the ignition and threw it into the distance.

Leon tried to make a grab for Christopher who threw Maxine in between them and ran into the darkness. Without thinking I gave chase. We ran and ran, all the time my lungs burning for oxygen and blood drying on my cheek, leaving my skin feeling burnt and painful and my body feeling wrecked from the blows I'd endured earlier.

I can't lose sight of him, I can't let him get away.

Soon I realised Christopher was running slower and slower. The injection was beginning to take effect and then I saw him collapse altogether. I ran up to his inert body.

Just a crumpled heap...nothing to be scared of now.

Then I started to shake, the fear catching up with me. I hadn't had time to feel the fear before but I did now and it didn't feel pleasant. I sat down next to

Christopher on that wintry October night and waited for the others to get there.

Suddenly a white van appeared out of nowhere, roaring down the street.

Oh shit!

It braked hard and two men jumped out, one with a gun. Smart black suits and shiny black sunglasses, their hair slicked back like movie stars.

"Get in the back of the van!" one of them shouted.

I got up, fear once again flowing deep within my body. I got into the darkness of the van. A few seconds later Christopher was dumped in also, and then the door was firmly shut with a metallic thud, like a tombstone being shut on a crypt.

I began to pray then. I heard Christopher stirring.

"Christopher!" I whispered as low as I could; he managed a grunt.

"Christopher!" I said again, more urgently. This time his arm gripped mine.

He's listening.

"Christopher, they're going to kill me because they want Lucifer to rule this world." My voice was shaking. "They want to destroy all that we hold dear."

"Fuck you!"

"Christopher, our *goodness, our hope and our love...*"

"I said, fuck you!"

And then I took the gamble, it was only a guess but something told me it might be true.

"Like the way your mother loved you, you went to the graveyard to summon a demon and your mum found out and tried to stop you. You know this as well as me. Your mum didn't commit suicide; it was the chief of demons, Lucifer himself, who took her life!"

A punch landed on my nose, breaking it and making my eyes water with pain. I reeled backwards from the blow, but before I had time to think another blow landed on me, sending me into oblivion and blackness.

Christopher

I awoke. The first thing I noticed was candles surrounding me on all sides. I counted six.

I looked down in the dim light and saw the lines of a pentagram etched out in chalk. I was sitting in the centre of the pentagram; my arms and feet were tied. I saw a dark shape standing over me and knew it to be Christopher. Some way off I could hear a low murmur. I looked and in the darkness saw the two men: the Gods of the Dark Moon.

"Christopher you've got to listen to me".

I felt spit land on my face. I ignored it.

"You are getting in too deep. Once you kill me Lucifer will possess your body and you won't be around anymore. Lucifer will rule this world in your body."

I saw his hands twitch and from the dim light saw uncertainty in his eyes.

"No, you're lying," he said, "he's promised to make me a god."

"Lucifer doesn't keep his promises," I said, trying to stop my voice form shaking.

"No… I don't believe you".

"Think about your mother who loved you, you know as well as me it wasn't suicide. Lucifer had one of his agents murder her because she was going to stop you from doing what you are about to do."

Christopher paused for a long second. Then I heard a soft sobbing sound. He was crying, maybe for the second time in years, maybe for the second time since he was seventeen.

"Quick, Christopher, undo my bonds, we need to get out of here fast."

I thought he was going to refuse me, and waited for what seemed like an eternity for a response, but nothing, just a soft sobbing. I prayed the men from the Gods of the Dark Moon wouldn't hear him.

"Christopher, come on. Please," I said, praying for a breakthrough.

"How do you know my mum was murdered?" he asked suddenly, and I gave the best answer I could think of.

"Christopher, your mum was religious and she loved you. She wouldn't have committed suicide and left you, you know that as well as me."

"It did come as a shock to me," he sobbed. "I was shocked and couldn't believe it at the time."

"Your mother was strong; she wouldn't have taken her own life, she loved you. She would have made sure that she stayed around to look after you."

"It broke her heart when father left." He wiped his eyes, the sobs stopping slightly. "She could never speak to me about it… Her prayers to God had gone unanswered. It was truly horrible being so poor and it was then that I met the people from the Gods of the Dark Moon. They helped me when no one else would…"

The sobs started again.

"Christopher, they used you, they don't care about you. They're only after what they can get out of you. You are sensitive to psychic phenomena like I am, that's why they chose you to work for them. You mum didn't kill herself; in your heart of hearts you know that. It was them, your fellow brothers, who put an end to her life, to keep you in the trap. A trap created by Satan to separate the weak and desperate from the love of God. Christopher, quick before they hear us talking and kill me, undo my bonds… please…"

No movement, no response nothing.

"Christopher… for your mother's sake and that little Asian kid. I am your brother… Please."

Suddenly something seemed to snap in Christopher. He moved and within a few seconds the bonds holding me were suddenly cut.

"We need to make our escape as fast and quietly as we possibly can."

There was a door just on the right a few metres away which I believed to be the exit, as it swayed lightly with the wind from outside.

Quietly but quickly I said to Christopher, "Give me the knife."

He did so and we made our way to the door; we were just passing through when it creaked and alerted the two men.

"Hey!" they screamed and were suddenly after us.

We ran out into the darkness, almost blind. I saw we were by the docks and had been in an old derelict warehouse. They were giving chase. Large freight containers surrounded us on all sides.

A shot rang out and I looked back and saw Christopher was not there. I ducked behind a container and made a few left and right turns to lose my pursuers. I just hoped and prayed Christopher was alright and had made the decision to use the containers to also try and evade them.

I crouched down behind one of the containers and pulled out my mobile phone and quickly sent a text. I heard feet running and saw the light of a torch nearby, and got up and ran again.

They were following me and in the pitch black gloom I thought I had no chance.

The ground was muddy underfoot and then I realised that that was how they were following me.

After a few turns, I stood stock-still and retraced my footsteps carefully so as not to make any new prints but to keep my feet, which were now on tiptoe, within my footprints.

Soon I was crouched behind a container and I saw one of the men walk slowly past the side of me, slowly following my prints. The trick worked, but I knew I had to act now or he would see the footsteps end in emptiness and know what I had done. With all the force I could muster I charged him and thrust the knife into his back.

I suddenly felt my hands wet with blood. The figure went down, dropping the torch and the gun. I heard shots ring out in the distance. I picked up the gun and the torch and went back the way I had come.

I just prayed I wasn't too late to save Christopher.

I stood still, holding the torch, and then a few containers away I saw another torch coming towards me. I slowly took aim and let rip with the gun. Several shots at the torch. It fell to the ground.

I quickly ran towards the downed figure and saw he was dead, his pale face lying lifeless in the mud and dirt, his hair unkempt and part of his glasses lying broken under the weight of his arm.

I started to search for Christopher. After several minutes I found him, lying face down in the dirt and mud, a small puddle of blood had formed around him. I turned him over and took his pulse knowing even before I did that he was dead. In the distance I heard the sound of a car. I sat down with Christopher in the dark and wet, and just clutched his head to my chest. Tears welled deep in my eyes.

Christopher... Thank you...

I don't know how long after, but probably only a few

minutes later the text message I had sent worked, and Leon, Trisha and Natalie found me in the dirt with Christopher.

Leviathan

I sat at the controls of a B-29 super fortress bomber, better known by its nickname, the Bockscar, flying through the black clouds of Hell.

The calendar on the side wall of the bomber was open on August 6th 1945, the day the bomb known as Little Boy was dropped on Hiroshima.

I looked at my co-pilot, in his green military attire, same as me. His face had a pale sheen and his black lanky hair could be seen sticking out of his hat.

"We need to give these bastards what for!" he said. "They steal all that is good from us and corrupt it."

I sighed, understanding the sentiment.

"We will be over the target in two minutes," I said looking at the flight instruments, the red button to drop the Little Boy — the atom bomb — could be seen just a few inches away from my hands holding the flight-stick.

All I have to do is lift the plastic see-through top and push the button and Lucifer and his minions won't ever trouble us again.

"I know how you feel, the tortured nights I have spent fearing Lucifer and his minions have played havoc with my mind, and the death of Christopher," I sighed again.

"Lucifer represents all that is bad in the world, he is the root cause of all the pain and suffering in the world," said my co-pilot.

But I felt a tinge of annoyance. It wasn't Lucifer but man who had accepted him into their lives and let their desires control them.

I looked below through the thick black clouds which were now dissipating and I saw the fires of Hell below, glowing a spectral orange. Burnt-out buildings where Lucifer and his minions lived could be seen. I looked at the instruments.

We will be over the drop spot in one minute.

My co-pilot continued, "The evil in Lucifer has wrecked too many lives."

What about the evil in man?

"Lucifer is evil and he is the reason man fell from the grace of God."

There is good and bad in all of us, even Lucifer was good at one time according to the scriptures.

"He must be stopped. We must put an end to him and his minions once and for all."

We can all fall but we can also all be redeemed, Christopher taught me that much.

The instruments indicated we would be flying over the target spot in less than thirty seconds. I looked at my co-pilot.

Who is he? What is he doing here? I know I'm dreaming.

Suddenly we were over the target spot.

"Drop the bomb," he said. I lifted the plastic see-through cover and rested my finger in mid-air above the button.

Something stopped me; a thought.

Evil cannot defeat evil... Only love can defeat evil.

I looked at him again, his gaze bore through me with its deep cavernous stare.

"I'm not going to drop it," I said, suddenly coming to a decision.

His face frowned, "What about all the evil in the world? What about Christopher, his mum, your soul and all the patients at St Mark's hospital?"

"Evil cannot defeat evil," I returned.

Those eyes! No it couldn't have been, were they suddenly slit and green?

"Drop it now, we only have a few seconds before we fly over the target spot."

I looked down onto the fires below and felt nothing but sadness and sorrow for the denizens of Hell and even for Lucifer himself.

"I won't," I said more assertively and suddenly we had overflown the target spot.

The co-pilot unstrapped his seat belt and headed towards the back of the plane. I got up to see what he was doing. He strapped on a parachute and walked towards the door, and suddenly air rushed through the cabin of the plane as he jumped out, down into Hell.

I struggled my way to the door and shut it. I then went to the back of the plane and looked at the five-tonne bomb and saw something that puzzled me, where the name of the bomb should have read 'Little Boy' it said simply 'Soul'. *My soul.*

If I had dropped my bomb I would have sent my soul into the fields of Hell itself but I hadn't, and thereby had saved myself. I sighed deeply and felt light-headed.

I awoke. There was a ringing sound in my ears, which I now realised was my mobile. I pulled it out from under my pillow.

"Hi Zahid!"

It was Natalie.

"Hi Natalie!" I said, feeling happy.

"Zahid, I've been thinking it was really brave the way you tackled Christopher and the Gods of the Dark Moon the other day and I want to give you another chance, so I'm asking you out on another date."

"Yes!" I screamed, feeling so elated.

"I'd love to, Natalie," I said into the phone, now breathless as my heart beat rapidly in my ears and my breath came in short gasps.

The Second Date

I had freshened up and dressed smartly and now I waited for Natalie at exactly the same meeting spot as last time.

It was late October and the darkness surrounded me, but I felt no fear of the dark. I had conquered that with the death of the men from the Gods of the Dark Moon and the outwitting of Leviathan in the plane.

Now I faced a much more subtle challenge. Natalie and her beautiful mind and body I knew would test my resources to the limit.

I saw her arrive in her black dress and walk up to me. As before she looked stunning with her blue eye-shadow, pale lithe arms and shapely waist. I took a deep breath and put the thought of what I wanted to do with her to the back of my mind.

We entered the pizza restaurant and sat at the same table as last time. I looked at her and smiled and she smiled back.

So far so good.

The waiter arrived and we ordered one large pizza.

"It was really brave the way you handled Christopher and the Gods of the Dark Moon."

"Thank you," I replied feeling pleased. "You did really well too. If you hadn't got that injection into Christopher when you did we would never have stopped him."

"Yes, it was really sad about what happened to him," she said looking down. "Especially after what he did to try and save himself, and you."

Tears welled in my eyes but I fought them down.

"Yes, he wasn't a bad guy really; I just wish we could have done more for him. When's the funeral?" I asked.

"Friday 9:30am at St Mark's Cemetery."

"Good, I will be there".

"We're all going, all the staff from Ward Four."

The waiter put the pizzas down and left. Natalie smiled and we both started to eat. For a while we ate in silence, simply happy to be in each other's company and with our own thoughts. It certainly had been a turbulent few weeks.

And then I dropped the bombshell.

"Natalie, there's something I need to tell you."

She looked up.

"I can't work at the hospital with what's happened anymore. So I decided to leave. I'm handing my notice in on Monday".

"Awww… Zahid, I'm really sad to hear that. We're all going to miss you, you really settled in as a valuable member of the team."

Then she reached out her hand and touched mine which was resting lazily on the table.

"Let's order dessert," she said.

I had chocolate ice cream and she had a banana split. Then we exited the restaurant my hand still feeling warm from her touch. As I waited to say our goodbyes the moment stretched out and then Natalie said it.

"Follow me in your car, you can come to my place for a bit."

I beamed back.

"OK, no probs," and was suddenly wondering for a bit of what?

After a few minutes' driving we arrived at Natalie's house. I entered and sat down on the sofa; she sat next to me. The lights were dim and Natalie put some soft background music on and got me a glass of wine.

We talked for a while about things in general and then I made my move and she didn't resist. I felt her hot lips on mine, her hot breath on mine and her soft skin on mine. I ran her fine delicate hair through my fingers and slowly we undressed each other.

The sex was incredible, it was truly out of this world and waking up on the sofa in the morning with Natalie wrapped around me as exhausted as I was made me feel like I was the happiest man alive.

I got up and made her a drink of tea and got some biscuits. We sat staring and talking softly like newlyweds on their honeymoon.

I felt so much bliss then that I regretted the decision to leave as it would mean I wouldn't be able to see Natalie as much as I wanted; but last night, in the throes of passion, she had promised me that we could still go out.

The sparkling sunshine made its weak way through the living room curtains and we sat and talked late into the afternoon without getting dressed.

We talked and talked. I felt I had never been with anyone before who I had fallen for so utterly and felt so close to. It made me so happy when she said that she felt exactly the same way.

A little later we both got dressed, ordered a Chinese takeaway and then fell back to lovemaking once again.

Pure bliss...

The Funeral

It was a bright late October morning.

The sun shone but the rest of the weather was dreary. The wind was cold and harsh although there were lulls every now and again. The rain which seemed to be unable to make its mind up about itself was cold and merciless.

We all stood gathered around the coffin of Christopher Haunton. There were no relatives present, his mother had been his only living relative and she had died many years ago.

The priest went over Christopher's life, how he had given joy to so many people who had known him although he had been afflicted with a terrible illness early in life, and now hoped that he would find rest at last.

I thought about the short time I had known him and realised what a remarkable character he had been. Always thinking, always questioning.

I was sad that my time at the hospital was now **over, but after his death I just couldn't work there** anymore. I hoped the others knew and understood this.

I looked now at Natalie who stood opposite me in her mourning clothes. She smiled nervously and quickly looked away.

At least some joy had come out of my job. I felt like I had grown as a person and was now more able to appreciate the beauty of life all around me more than I had previously.

I looked up and saw two blackbirds in a tree nearby, just sitting in the bright sun and dreary weather.

Life is so simple, why do others always have to complicate it?

Trisha stood next to me and Leon opposite her on the other side of the grave, their expressions sombre.

"Dust to dust, ashes to ashes," said the priest sprinkling soil onto the coffin.

Leon, Trisha, Natalie and I lifted the coffin with the straps and gently lowered it into the damp earth.

Goodbye Christopher and thank you for what you have given me; a second chance at life. Hope wherever you are, you are happy.

Slowly the others started to melt away. I stood there, I don't know how long.

Eventually I turned to go and found Natalie waiting for me.

Miss Akisha Moon

Natalie was hiding something, I just knew it.

We had been together for a week now and there would always be something about her, like she was on the verge of telling me something but then would pull back at the last minute. To be honest it was really beginning to infuriate me.

So in the bar at 11pm, when we were both a little drunk but not too drunk, I confronted her.

"Natalie, what are you hiding from me?"

She paused. I could see she was unsure of what to say. I stood my ground and stared straight at her.

"I can't... I can't say just yet," she said into my ear.

I felt totally exhausted and worn out after everything that had happened over the last few weeks. **I didn't have the patience to play games or wait** patiently for snippets of what Natalie was hiding from me.

Is it an affair? Has she gone off me? Are her ***parents ill? Whatever it is, I've had enough of this. I*** *need answers*, I thought.

I grabbed her hands in mine but not too forcefully.

"Tell me."

"I need to go to the toilet."

She pulled her hands away and was gone.

I sat on the stool and waited for her to come back, thinking about what I would say to her, and then I saw her. She took my breath away. Slim, busty, blond, blue eyes and a candour which just grabbed my heart.

She came up to the table and put her empty drink down. I just stared like a schoolkid, thrilled by the hint of teenage sexuality. She paused a second, looked at me and winked.

I suddenly got up and found myself holding her hand, leaning into her as I tried to talk over the sound of the music and shout into her ear.

I saw her smile, press her lean fit body into mine and place her lips on mine, her tongue pushed deep into my mouth and it was one of the nicest feelings I had ever had. I placed one hand on her slim behind and another cupped her left breast and squeezed. She pushed me back against the stool and I felt our groin areas, wishing we weren't wearing clothing.

Suddenly I thought about Natalie and knew she couldn't see me with this girl. I pushed her off me, which was no easy task with me being so turned on. She lifted her hand and placed a card in my shirt pocket and disappeared the next instant into the throng of bodies all around me.

Just then Natalie came back looking tired and fraught, she had redone her mascara but I could tell she had been crying and hated myself in that instant for letting my desires get the better of me.

"I'm not feeling too well, I'm going home."
We'd taken a taxi to the club together and now I felt that we should end the night together too, but this

could be my opportunity to go after Miss Teenage Sexuality and have a great night.

But I knew my conscience wouldn't let me so I exited the club with Natalie and waited outside in the drizzly rain for our taxi. Natalie had a lot on her mind and was in no mood for conversation.

The taxi dropped her off and as I sat in the back I pulled out the card the girl had given me and read:

Miss Akisha Moon
Love the beauty in you
Reflexology and Beauty Therapist.
Call 07742 60948

I thought about throwing the card away but couldn't; there was something about her that I just couldn't or didn't want to let go of. I placed the card back into my pocket knowing that I would call her tomorrow and be done with Natalie's secrets once and for all if she didn't reveal them to me sooner rather than later.

… Unknown to Zahid, Miss Akisha Moon exited the bar soon after Natalie and him, and was picked up by a white van with a driver who wore dark sunglasses, had hair slicked back like a movie stars and a dark suit…

Natalie's truth

Natalie and I sat on a park bench in bright early morning sunshine. The air was still, not warm but not cold either, just mild.

I had called for her and we had gone for our regular walk like we usually did and I finally began to think that we were getting close, really close.

Natalie had been holding something back from me I knew, but I was happy to let her tell me when she felt able. I wasn't going to force the issue.

"Zahid, there's something I want to tell you but I'm scared about what you will think of me."

"Natalie I won't judge you, you know that."

She paused, looking at the ground and then she said it in an emotionless robotic voice. She let it all out and I listened and took it all in.

"When I was seventeen, I was in love with Dave. He'd just passed his driving test and his dad had bought him a brand new Golf GTI. He took me for a spin."

She stopped, tears coming to her eyes.

"It's OK Natalie," I said, stroking her hand in mine.

She continued.

"We were coming off the slip road and we saw the truck too late. The car ploughed into the truck, Dave didn't survive and I've been battling post-traumatic stress disorder and depression ever since."

Tears streamed down her cheeks, and I felt my eyes were also moist. I clasped her hand even tighter in mine and she leaned her head into my chest and shoulder.

"Dave still haunts me, whenever I meet someone new he always pops up and makes me feel guilty for going with anyone else other than him," she said through her crying.

"He's in the past, Natalie, you were in love, but he's gone now and you need to move on," I said, tears now streaming down my cheeks.

Suddenly she started to sob uncontrollably and clasped her arms around me tightly.

"You need to put the past to rest," I said.

She didn't answer but I knew something in Natalie had changed; she had taken her first steps to recovery by letting me into her secret. I knew with my help she would overcome her guilt and shame at going with someone else even though Dave was no longer around.

"I will go with you if you'd like to see Dave's grave, and be there while you talk to him. Tell him you still love him but now need to get on with your life, that your grief has held you back for too many years."

"Thank you," she said simply and quietly as we hugged each other in the bright early morning sun.

The End

About the Author

Zahid Zaman is a 32-year-old psychology graduate who lives in England and likes reading books by Ursula Le Guin, David Gemmell and Stephen King. He started writing at an early age and has completed forty-six short horror and science fiction stories.

He has won best psychological horror and best science fiction tie on the *demonminds* website in 2003; his short story titled 'Dark Woods' appeared in print in *Halloween 2.0*, published by Cyber Pulp.

He also had a story printed in a competition held by his local library. His story 'Moonlight Sonata' was sold to the magazine *Alternate Species* and was also anthologised in *Project Contagion*.

His story entitled 'Eternity' was voted as one of the best stories of 2004 on the *Aphelion* website and another tale titled 'Digital Reality' has been published in the print anthology *Tabloid Purposes 3*.

His story titled 'Tulia Bellona: the Serial Killer's Daughter' was the lead story in the print publication *Ethereal Gazette*.

If you have any comments or questions about this book, please don't hesitate to contact Zahid at dynamicink09@yahoo.co.uk. Writers love to hear from their readers.

BV - #0157 - 080222 - C0 - 203/127/7 - PB - 9780993526565 - Matt Lamination